"I DON'T BELIEVE YOU, JOY!"

Brett's dark eyes clouded. He rose abruptly, towering over her quivering form, his face contorted with pain and anger. "You felt the same way I did down on the beach. Don't bother to deny it!

"I don't want to have a casual affair with you. I want to *marry* you—yet you treat my proposal like an insult. I can't stand much more of this torture—being with you and not having you.

"Tonight I thought you were finally ready to climb out of your dark cave and join the rest of the human race. But I was wrong—very wrong! Well, you needn't worry. I won't be around to intrude on your privacy. You can be alone to your heart's content.

"Now, please excuse me if I don't escort you to your room. Since you are so intent on doing things on your own, you can find your way, I'm sure. Good night!"

Brett's words, like physical blows, forced the breath from Joy's body, leaving her battered and speechless. As she watched him stalking angrily from the courtyard, she was faced with the most staggering realization of all—that she did, indeed, love Brett McCort!

FOUNTAIN OF LOVE

Velma S. Daniels
and Peggy E. King

Serenade
BOOKS
of the Zondervan Publishing House
Grand Rapids, Michigan

FOUNTAIN OF LOVE
Copyright © 1983 by The Zondervan Corporation
Grand Rapids, Michigan

Library of Congress Cataloging in Publication Data
Daniels, Velma Seawell.
  Fountain of love.

  I. King, Peggy E.   II. Title.
PS3554.A567F6   1983   813'.54   83-6707
ISBN 0-310-50012-5

The Scripture text used is that of the New International Version, copyright
© 1978 by the New York International Bible Society. Used by permission.

Edited by Anne Severance
Designed by Kim Koning

Printed in the United States of America

83 84 85 86 87 88 89 / 10 9 8 7 6 5 4 3 2 1

All characters are fictitious, with the exception of employees of the Boca
Hotel and The Chambered Nautilus. Care has been given to describing
accurately the Boca complex and our appreciation goes to Sue Schaal,
Director of Public Relations, for her gracious and courteous assistance.
Special thanks to Mrs. Lenora Hewett, Helen Carr, and Monsieur
Berlien—whose names appear in the first chapter.

To my husband, Dexter Daniels, Jr., my source of never-ending love

—VSD

and

For those who cared enough during the dark days to light up my life with love and joy

—PEK

"For there is in every creature a fountain of life which, if not choked back by stones and other dead rubbish, will create a fresh atmosphere, and bring to life fresh beauty."

Margaret Fuller (Ossoli)
1810–1850

CHAPTER 1

THROUGH A BRIDAL-VEIL MIST, the silver Mercedes sped into the night—the laughing couple inside oblivious to the danger looming just around the next bend in the freeway. Suddenly—out of nowhere—jackknifed across the rain-slick road—was a huge fuel tanker, forming a solid, immovable object. The mist lifted momentarily as the driver of the silver sports car looked on in horror. There was a squeal of brakes and a frantic turn of the wheel before impact. A split second later, both vehicles were engulfed in flames . . .

"No! No! Stop! Please stop!" Joy Lawrence screamed, her fists clenched, tears raining down her cheeks. Her eyes flew open as she pulled herself to a sitting position in bed, her slim body beneath the delicate fabric of her nightgown damp with perspiration.

The ribbon of moonlight filtering through her bedroom window told Joy it was still nighttime. Over two hundred and fifty nights since the accident. At least a hundred nightmares as cruelly vivid as this one.

"Stop it! Stop it!" she shrieked. But there was no one to hear her except Granny, her calico cat, who was deep in her mice-and-cream dream world.

The outburst shattered the last remnants of Joy's terror. She lay spent in the gray shadows of the pre-dawn, afraid that the nightmare would recur if she went back to sleep. She threw the covers aside and stepped from her bed, hours before her sleep was satisfied.

She flipped on her bedside lamp. Restless and distraught, Joy's eyes darted around the room. The familiarity of her surroundings temporarily comforted her.

As one of Atlanta's leading dress designers, Joy had decorated her small, five-room cottage with a romantic flavor—reminiscent of English countryside hospitality. A plush, mauve carpet covered the floors throughout the house, providing a soft backdrop for both the muted tones and startling decorator colors she had chosen.

Joy's bed, her own original design, had been featured in *House and Garden* magazine. She had worked with a master craftsman to create the look of a window box of flowering violets. The base of the bed was made of wood and stained with a black matte finish. The open, ruffled canopy was a veritable garden of hand-stitched purple violets. The soft curtains were drawn back with pull-cord streamers of pastel green silk to simulate the stems of the violets. She had appliqued garlands of violets on the bedlinens.

A petit point picture in lavender yarn on a creamy background carried out the delicate floral motif with the embroidered words: "Forget-me-not, the bluebell, and that Queen of Secrecy, the violet . . ." Keats.

Nestled in the corner of the studio bedroom was Joy's oversized working table of pristine white flagstone, providing an interesting background for living things—a brass urn of feathery ferns. Shimmering fabric samples and sketches of party clothes for her clients were strewn over the surface of the desk. The list of those who engaged Joy's services to design their clothes read like the *Who's Who* of Atlanta.

Joy pulled her parfait pink robe around her shoulders and sat down at her worktable. Perhaps an hour or two of hard work would dispel the memory of the terrible dream. She fingered the drawings of two of the gowns she had recently designed for the leading social event of the year—the Piedmont Hospital Ball. The gowns had been designed for two of her favorite customers, Mrs. Lenora Hewett and Colonel Carr's wife, Helen.

She looked with decided approval at the Hewett design. She had used scarlet satin, richly embellished with exotic Persian flowers. Mrs. Hewett left all the details of style and color up to Joy. Her only request was that the gown and her walking cane must match. Joy had chosen a rich walnut stick and had taken it to Monsieur Berlien at the Berlien Jewelers on the Park. Monsieur had studded the walking cane with rubies. The total effect of the ensemble defied description.

Mrs. Hewett's breath had caught in mid-air at the first sight of her ensemble. She didn't speak for a few moments and then she exclaimed, "Joy Lawrence, you are a genius! You have the creativity of your mother, and the class of Coco Chanel, Dior, and Schiaparelli all rolled into one gorgeous lady!" Joy had delighted in her friend's satisfaction.

Mrs. Carr's ball gown was, of course, very different. Each of Joy's designs was unique—never duplicating a single feature of another design. She smiled now as she recalled Helen's reaction the first time she saw the sketch for her gown. In lady-like fashion, she had nearly exploded! "Joy, I didn't think I had to tell you after all these years . . . you know my gowns are always to be white, beige, or cream. My goodness, that does not anymore look like me than . . .''

"Now, now, Mrs. Carr. You are under no obligation to accept these drawings or my ideas. I just thought with your divine figure, your peach-blossom complexion, and the dancing lights in your strawberry-blonde hair, it was high time you selected something not resembling a lady quail," Joy retorted as light-heartedly as possible.

Mrs. Carr was a bit taken aback by Joy's reply and decided to trust the expertise of the young designer. The gown was of glorious silk gazar, as deeply and mysteriously purple as a precious amethyst. The low-backed silhouette gave it an air of tender femininity, embraced by an orchid capelet. On the day after the creation was delivered to the Carr home, a note came to The Boutique from Colonel Carr by special messenger. It read simply: "Helen's gown —pure ecstacy!"

Usually Joy could lose herself for hours in the dreamy images of her drawings, but not tonight. Normally her cottage was a secure haven. Tonight she felt as though the walls were closing in on her, suffocating her.

Perhaps a few deep breaths of the crisp night air would balance her teetering emotions. Joy removed the bolt lock on the sliding-glass doors which disappeared between the bedroom and the trellised area opening into a mini-porch. She stepped out barefooted and inhaled the chilly March air. Exhale . . . inhale . . . exhale. She felt calmer, more relaxed. She went back into her bedroom and locked the doors. Suddenly the nightmarish fear swept over her again and she felt she had to get out of the room . . . out of the house.

She grabbed a pair of white, wrinkled slacks and a multi-striped blouse that was thrown over the chair. Quickly she slipped into her tennis shoes without even bothering to tie the laces. She scooped the cat out of her warm basket and dashed out to her car. Granny curled up in the seat beside her mistress and went right back to sleep. Joy turned the ignition key and her red Mustang convertible began to hum as she shoved it into reverse and backed recklessly out of her open garage. A fast drive with her windows down might help her to forget. At least, perhaps it would steady her rapid pulse and lift the depression that had crushed down upon her.

I'm losing my mind, Joy thought. *Otherwise why would I be driving sixty miles an hour at four o'clock in the morning—going nowhere!*

Even at that hour the city of Atlanta was teeming with life. She careened around the corner of Peachtree Street and flipped off her automatic cruise control. Her car coasted back to the acceptable speed limit. The spectacular Hyatt Regency with its glass tower addition loomed ahead. Her spirits were buoyed briefly as she thought of the exotic birds and the glass elevators in the atrium-lobby. But the uplift in Joy's mood was short-lived.

"Am I crazy? What is happening to me?" she cried out in desperation. But there was not a sound except the steady breathing of the cat.

Now as she drove through the streets of Atlanta lined with darkened houses, she wondered how any of the population could be sleeping peacefully. The city sounds of the early morning—the clatter of milk and produce trucks, garbage vehicles, mail carts, a few tipsy party-goers singing as they toddled down the sidewalks—only added to her restlessness.

Slowly Joy began to reconstruct in her mind the events of the previous evening. What had she done to trigger the nightmare? She had taken a languorous bubble bath and settled down with a romantic novel, *Cherry Blossom Prin-*

13

cess, by her friend Marjorie Holmes. On page 124 she had read, "Little girls your age should be in bed." She smiled to herself and marked the page so that she could pick up where she had stopped reading. She was no little girl, but the advice was applicable to big girls as well.

That was the last thing she remembered before falling asleep. And now here she was, too tired and confused to think clearly. She turned on the radio to see if some early morning music would calm her nerves, then reached over to rub her pet's soft fur.

Joy had found Granny the day she moved into her cottage. The cottage had originally belonged to Joy's parents and was nestled in a secluded corner on the grounds of the estate. Faire and Townsend Lawrence had intended it to be used as a recreation house, but it seemed an equally delightful spot for the grandparents when they came for a visit. Thereafter the small cottage was called "Granny's flat." That's why, on the night Joy had found the half-starved calico cat in the shrubbery, the name had stuck. And when she noticed the cat's unusual eyes—one, a brilliant blue; the other, as yellow as topaz—she knew Granny had found a home. "Why, you belong here with me!" Joy had exclaimed. "Topaz is my birthstone, and you are certainly the best birthday present I've ever received."

Not only did Granny provide her with companionship, but often with excuses. Joy smiled to herself as she thought of the number of times young men had telephoned her for a date, and she had explained coyly, "Sorry, but I have to stay home with Granny tonight." She always hoped they would never discover that Granny was not an adorable little old lady, but rather a peculiar, odd-eye calico cat. Granny returned Joy's pamperings with her own brand of love— purrs and soft, furry rubs against Joy's ankles.

The night ride for cat and mistress had been going on for

more than an hour when Joy noticed that the gas gauge was registering almost empty. Nearing the Druid Hills section of Atlanta, she decided the wisest thing to do was to stop at The Boutique and wait until morning. She made two right turns and parked her Mustang under the porte-cochere. The cat peeked up over the window to see what was happening, then curled up and promptly went back to sleep.

Joy squinted in the semi-darkness. The March sky was beginning to lighten a bit with splashes of gray and pink stripes. The dove-colored pre-dawn matched Joy's mood. She continued to study the shoppe, a wedding present from her father to her mother. She had made few changes since she had become the proprietor.

Will I ever stop missing them? she thought. They had given such permanence and substance to her life. Somehow they had implanted their strong Christian beliefs in her heart from the time she was old enough to understand. They had guided her without dictating, and this had allowed her to grow in her faith as she had grown physically. "I wonder if I ever told them enough how much I appreciated them?" she spoke aloud. "I'm a lucky woman—wonderful parents, this beautiful shoppe, the best clients in Atlanta, and my friend Ellen to help me run it. Well, if I'm so blessed, then what's the matter with me? Why am I behaving like some kind of immature brat?"

Joy picked up her cat, cradled her lovingly in her arms and made her way to the nearest side door. She unlocked the door and turned off the alarm system to prevent setting it off as she entered. The serenity of the posh interior was in direct contrast to the seething emotions inside her.

She put the snoozing cat on a nearby footstool and then sat down at her desk. She ran her fingers through her tangled hair. Her emotions were still ricocheting off her rib cage and into the pit of her stomach like a pair of racquet balls. She was not accustomed to wasting time. But she had no interest in doing anything that required effort. She rested her arm on the desk and laid her head down to wait for Ellen. Sleep took over for at least a moment.

CHAPTER 2

ELLEN TURNER COULDN'T shake the uneasy feeling that had hovered over her since the wee hours of the morning. In all of her fifty-two years she had never felt so disturbed, although she could not think of a proper reason. Her breathing reflected her nervousness as she hummed short snatches of familiar tunes. Her stride was long for her petite frame, which she kept firm and lithe with regular exercise. She raced along at almost a jogging tempo.

Gray shadows played through the giant oaks that lined the boulevard. The sun, struggling to peek through, rested its first beams on the oversized azalea bushes and dogwood trees. Atlanta had always been Ellen's home. Though she had looked at these same trees, these same bushes, these same shops every morning for as long as she could remember, she had never tired of them.

She tried to think of little things—like the letters she must mail, the fur boots in the window of Rich's, the milk she needed to pick up after work. But the wary feeling that sat now on her shoulders crowded out her thoughts.

Click—click—click. The sound of her boot heels was all Ellen could hear, along with the muffled sound of early morning traffic. The leftovers of winter in the form of a chilly frost had turned the Georgia clay to iron. The sidewalks were merely a thin, piecrust topping for the hardened soil.

She stopped at the corner stand to purchase her usual newspaper from old Mr. Johnson. The date on the paper read: Tuesday, March 1.

"Good morning, Mrs. Turner."

"Good morning to you, Mr. Johnson."

"Ma'am, it seems like you and I are the only folks up early this morning. When it's nippy, folks hate to roll out of bed," he chuckled good-naturedly.

"I don't blame them a bit. But I like to get to The Boutique early and tidy things up before Miss Lawrence arrives at noon," replied Ellen.

"Noon! Folks waste the best part of the day when they lazy around until noon."

Ellen searched in her purse for some coins.

"Lazy? Well, if there is one thing Joy Lawrence *isn't*, it's lazy," Ellen retorted. "She's just like her mother. She gets up before the sun. Then she does some of her dress-designing in the quiet of her home before she comes to the shoppe. No, Mr. Johnson, Joy doesn't have a lazy bone in her body."

"Oh, no ma'am, I didn't mean Miss Joy was lazy. Never was finer folks in this world than the Lawrences. Mr. Townsend was the kindest, most generous man I ever met. Sometimes he'd buy a paper and tip me a five-spot. I'll always remember the day they had that terrible automobile accident. When I heard about it, I cried. I had lost a good friend—me, just a nobody and him a mighty big man. But he called me 'friend.' When my wife was sick, well, he sent

18

his doctor to see her. She'd have been dead if it hadn't been for Mr. Townsend.

"Rich? Sure they was. But they was never ones to flaunt it or brag. Seems like they had more fun helping other folks with their money than they did spending it on themselves. Beatenes' thing I ever run across. Nope, there aren't many folks around like the Lawrences. Too bad, too."

Ellen hoped the old man's chatter would soon come to a stop. Memories were hard for Ellen. But no such luck. Mr. Johnson took a deep breath to choke back the tears in his quivering voice.

"Yessirree, I remember it like it was yesterday. And it's been pretty nearly a year. The newspaper called him a 'self-made financial wizard.' And Mrs. Lawrence, she was as pretty as a picture. The newspaper said her name was Faire—Faire Lawrence. Well, her mama sure named her right. Sure is nice you and Miss Joy kept Mrs. Lawrence's dress shoppe. I know she's looking down mighty proud."

One thing about Mr. Johnson, he surely was a "talker." Ellen was having trouble finding her coins through the tears that had brimmed over when the old man began to talk about Townsend and Faire Lawrence. She found her money, counted it out, picked up a newspaper, and put it in her carry-all bag.

The traffic light signaled "Walk" and she hastened to cross the street. The conversation with Mr. Johnson had done nothing to perk up her spirits. She had tried for the sake of herself and Joy not to dwell on the deaths of her friends. Ellen had plunged into a therapeutic frenzy of work. She had become Joy's surrogate mother, her best friend, her business partner.

"If I had been fortunate enough to have a daughter of my own, I would not love her any more than I do that girl," she muttered as she walked.

And so, Joy and Ellen—one, young and vivacious; one, middle-aged and lonely—reached out to each other in their mutual loss. Sharing their grief somehow made it more bearable.

Ellen rounded the corner leading to The Boutique. *Where have all the years gone?* She continued her reminiscing as she hurried along. She smiled to herself. She had to admit that she was comfortable and pleased with her life.

Joy and The Boutique are my life now, she mused.

Ellen's thoughts were still skittering about when the shoppe came into view. Old oaks formed an umbrella over the green-and-white canopy that led from the street to the heavy, walnut door of the salon. A small, bronze plate read simply, "The Boutique."

Ellen put her key in the lock at the same moment she spotted Joy's Mustang in the carport. Her spirits soared like sunshine. She could hardly wait to tell Joy about the new orders they had already received since the weekend ball. Their work calendar rotated around three major Atlanta social events: the prestigious Piedmont Hospital Ball held annually on the last Friday in January, at the Piedmont Driving Club; the Crawford W. Long Hospital Benefit Ball, held at the Cherokee Town Club in February; and the late summer Debutante Ball.

She turned her key and stepped onto the plush, pink Oriental rug. The rug unified the rooms of the salon with a muted variant of the luscious color. A love seat with deep cushions of rose velvet added to the elegance. A scroll-topped armoire dominated the entry, and an antique cherry cabinet displayed an assortment of miniature porcelains, among them Joy's favorite—the Boehm pink perfection camellia.

"It's me!" Ellen called cheerily. There was no reply, but the faint scent of Joy's perfume permeated the rooms.

"It's me, dear. I'm going to open the draperies and I'll be right there."

Still there was no reply. It was nothing more than an unsteady sensation. But Ellen didn't like it.

The sounds of silence were eerie. She could have heard a pin drop, a page turn, a muffled sigh. But there was nothing. Ellen quickly turned on the lights. She forgot all about opening the draperies as she hurried to the back of the shoppe.

Her breath almost stopped. Joy was slumped over her desk, her shoulders shaking with inaudible sobs.

Ellen's eyes widened in disbelief. Feverishly she unbuttoned her blue coat, kicked her sturdy walking boots to one side, and rushed over to Joy.

"What is it, dear?" she asked.

Joy, always immaculately groomed, was a mess. She was as pale as alabaster. Her eyelids were swollen as she looked up at her friend. Large, unchecked tears came in floods down her cheeks and soaked her rumpled blouse. She looked as if she had slept in her clothes.

"I—I don't know, Ellen! I feel crazy . . . almost like I'm having a nervous breakdown. I'm coming apart inside!" The buzz saw whining in her head was so loud that she was surprised Ellen couldn't hear it.

Ellen waited, not interrupting to calm the sobs that came now in huge gulps. When the crying subsided, she said quietly, "You are not having a nervous breakdown. You are not crazy. You are not coming apart. Joy Lawrence, you are just exhausted, bone-weary, fatigued," she emphasized. "You haven't done anything but work, work, work these past nine months. You haven't taken off one single holiday. Now, young lady, work is the best antidote for grief that I know anything about. But *overwork* is another thing. You are killing yourself."

The younger woman snuffled, blew her nose, and began to pour out her heart to her friend. "I had another of those awful nightmares, Ellen. I saw Mother and Daddy's car burst into flames when it struck the tanker, and no one could get them out! It was as clear as if I had been there and had seen it myself!"

Ellen was familiar with Joy's nightmares. She had spent more than one night comforting her young friend—hearing her out as she poured out her grief—preparing warm milk so that she could slip into dreamless sleep.

"What can I do to help?" Ellen coaxed.

"Nothing. I have to get myself together. No one can do it for me. I pray, but God seems so far away. Sometimes I think He's left me, too."

"Of course He hasn't! Joy, God is with you all the time. He was there last night. He is here now. You just *feel* far from Him because your mind and body are exhausted. He will never leave you and, when you get through this terrible ordeal, you will feel even closer to Him than before. I know you find that hard to believe now, but it will happen. Just remember that," she explained to Joy softly.

There was silence for what seemed like a very long time. Joy was the first to speak. Her voice quavered.

"I've had a long night to think about things—a lot of things. I need to get away for a while. What would you say if I took off a few days, maybe a couple of weeks. I hate myself. I don't feel like designing another gown. I even dread coming to The Boutique some days. Does any of this make sense?"

"Perfectly good sense!" Ellen affirmed. "I say *go*. What you need is a good dose of sunshine, sand, and sea. Don't worry about me. Granny and I will take care of everything. And for goodness' sakes, don't worry about this shoppe!"

Joy felt tiny fingers of relief creep up her spine, soothing taut nerves and muscles. Having made the decision, she was already beginning to feel better. She stood up suddenly. As she did, she caught her own reflection in the full-length mirror. she could not believe what she saw—raggedy lines across her salty, stained face; hair that had been combed with her fingers; wrinkled clothes.

"Is this really me?" she gasped.

Ellen laughed. "I'm afraid so. While you put yourself back together, I'll fix you a strong cup of coffee and a croissant. The society section of the paper should have the pictures of the Ball. Why don't you check?" Ellen put down the newspaper and disappeared into the kitchenette.

As Joy read the society news, noting with satisfaction the accuracy of the reporter's descriptions of the gowns, Ellen poured the coffee into a delicate Lenox china cup. She buttered the croissant and added a generous dollop of orange marmalade. She smiled at Joy. "I'm making your reservations this very morning."

"Where am I going?" Joy giggled.

"To Boca Raton, Florida, my dear. When you were just a little girl and visited there with your family, you would say, 'I love this place better than anywhere in the world. If I ever run away, you can find me in Boca Raton.' Now you are a big girl, and I say run away to Boca Raton!" Ellen threw her head back and laughed. Her laughter, like the tinkle of silver bells, was so like her mother's that Joy felt a momentary pang of nostalgia.

"It sounds perfect!" she said. "To tell you the truth, I'm glad I don't have to make another decision. My brain is as full of cobwebs as my hair is full of tangles," Joy called back over her shoulder as she went into the bathroom to freshen up. She could remember with fondness the Cloister—pink stucco, the soft glow of candlelight falling on old damask, warm hospitality.

She was in better spirits, though she didn't look a great deal better. Mechanically Joy tended to some paperwork at her desk. *Maybe tomorrow a new life will begin for Joy Lawrence,* she fantasized. *Off with the old me and on with the new.*

Tuesday was always a slow day in the shoppe. Both of the women welcomed the inactivity. Ellen answered the telephone, talked to a few customers who wandered in, and made Joy's airline reservations for the following morning. And as if in confirmation of her plans, there was a cancellation at the Cloister. Joy's room was in the west wing of the elegant, old hotel. So far, so good.

By five o'clock, they were already getting into the Mustang, with Ellen holding Granny. They drove home in silence. Both women were worn out from the strain of the day. They looked forward to hot showers and an early bedtime.

Joy was grateful for Ellen's company. Maybe she would be spared another nightmare tonight. At least she wouldn't feel the aching loneliness.

Joy's home was only a short drive from The Boutique and little more than fifteen minutes from the bustling center of Atlanta. The cottage, at the end of a tranquil, dogwood-lined lane, had an aura of romantic legend about it. Squirrels darted from tree to tree in an apparent 'welcome home' gesture. The cottage shone brightly since, in her hasty early-morning departure, Joy had forgotten to turn out the lights.

Ellen was as familiar with Joy's home as she was her own. She kept a nightgown, toothbrush, a set of electric curlers, and a complete change of clothes there. They came in handy when the two worked late, the weather was too bad to take the bus to the suburbs, or an emergency arose.

"Dear, why don't you go take a leisurely shower and put on your gorgeous panne velvet caftan with the rose, mint, and champagne stripes," Ellen suggested. "You always feel better when you wear it. I'll put linens on the sofa bed."

As she went into the living room, Ellen remembered how surprised she had been the first time she saw it after Joy's redecorating spree. With the mauve carpet, she had chosen as the predominant color a rich aubergine. Joy called it an "eggplant purple."

Noting her friend's expression, Joy had quickly said, "Before you say one single word, Ellen, let me show you how this shade looks at night in my magical world of candlepower!" Joy had always loved candlelight. She loved to eat by it, entertain by it and, as a little girl, she had insisted on having her own bedside candle to light each night.

Groupings of candles dominated the room now—short ones; chunky ones; tall, skinny tapers. There were so many that, when lighted, they almost matched the lamps with their luminosity. Depending on the natural, artificial, or candlelight, the aubergine changed dramatically. The effect was breathtakingly beautiful.

"One reason you are the best couturière in the business is your sensitivity to color," Ellen had congratulated Joy on her choice of the unusual combination.

As the older woman made the bed, Joy got her luggage out of the foyer closet. She decided on one large suitcase, a cosmetic carrier, and her airplane-weight hanging bag. Then she began to select her clothes for the trip, being careful to place sheets of crisp, scented tissue paper between her garments.

"I'm getting hungry," Ellen remarked. "How about one of your favorite Turner omelets oozing with cheese, a green salad, and a cup of tea?"

"Perfect!" Joy exclaimed. "You always know what I want even before I do."

She welcomed the few moments alone to pack, making mental notes of the accessories she would need. *That's another nice thing about Ellen. She senses when I need her and when I need to be alone,* Joy thought.

What should she wear on the plane? Boca Raton would be so much warmer than Atlanta. She was quick to decide on a tailored two-piece dress in teal blue, with shutter tucking, soft, inverted pleats, and a crisp tuxedo collar, with a kicky, black bow tie at the neckline. She chose a white mohair coat to carry on the plane and sling-back lizard sandals. She carefully attached her tiny, crystal cat pin with its topaz eye and 14-karat gold trim to the left shoulder of the bodice. The pin had been a gift from Ellen on her twenty-first birthday.

Joy's melancholy mood was still hanging heavy when she reached into her closet and accidentally brushed against the peach silk garment bag made especially for "the dress." She remembered with elation the circumstances behind the creation of this gown. She lifted the cover and, even though she had been the designer, she admired the work as if it had been done by someone else. Now her thoughts wandered back to the day in the shoppe when a flinty, old dowager had asked Joy, "Are you anywhere near the designer your mother was?"

When she had left without placing an order, Joy had said to Ellen, "There will never be another designer like Mother. You know that. After all, you and Mother were friends all of your lives, Ellen. She was able to create in each of her clients the joy of feeling feminine—to be pretty, desirable, and ladylike all at the same time. But I can't let *her* designs be *my* designs. I have some ideas of my own, and it's high time I expressed them!"

Ellen had not said a word. She had been waiting for the

26

moment when Joy would begin to assert her individuality. She knew, too, that if one human effort could help her young friend overcome her grief, it would be work.

Joy remembered how she had begun to sketch. She would make line drawings, then tear them up in frustration. For a while there was nothing but huge wads of paper cluttering her desk. But at least it was a beginning—both to get a hold on her own life and to breathe a fresh spirit into The Boutique.

"I know what I'll do!" Joy had exclaimed, on the verge of an inspiration. "I'll tell John I want to go to the Piedmont Hospital Ball this year—wearing an original design!"

"Good idea!" Ellen had replied. *"This* will be a first. For once, you won't just be there as 'window dressing' for *him."* Ellen's poor opinion of Joy's fiancé was obvious with every word.

"About John—" Ellen had continued, "do you really think the two of you share the same goals—the same beliefs? You love children, but John is too busy climbing the ladder to success to be much of a father, it seems to me. And what about his faith? Is he a believer like you—or is he drifting? Joy, have you ever considered all of these things —or are you just grasping for someone to hold onto since your mother and father died?"

The words, spoken in love, had stung nevertheless. Joy had paused, sensing that her friend was telling the truth— truth that Joy was not ready to hear. At the moment she had chosen to ignore the reference to John.

"Today I will design the most beautiful gown in the world," she bubbled. "There will never again be anything like this one. My reputation and yours, Ellen, rests on the reaction to this gown."

Sitting on the side of her bed, Joy still believed that the gown was one of the prettiest she had ever seen.

Black. I'm glad that I made the skirt of rich, black velvet.

27

Black is a color with intense impact—it says you are ex-pecting things to happen. How true that was when I wore it! She laughed aloud. Her thoughts continued. She had de-cided on the decoration for the bodice from a delicate bone china hairpin tray that her grandmother had given her. A cloisonné butterfly decorated the tray. When she had turned it over, tiny letters on the back spelled out, "Painted Lady." And that was what she had called the design for the gown.

She had chosen sheer, Parisian silk mesh, nearly invisible to the naked eye, for the bodice. And then with an artist's eye, she had begun to work, tracing in chalk on the silk mesh a twelve-by-twelve-inch butterfly. She measured and pinned the pattern to the bodice. From wingtip to wingtip, it spanned the entire front of the gown. Each section of the wings was sewn with a single hue of tiny crystals. Divisions of flaming orange, rich purple, sunflower yellow, hot crim-son, sky blue, and parrot green crystals transformed the butterfly design into a fantasy. Joy had then used tiny whis-pers of 14-karat gold thread to form the antennae of the butterfly. She had slipped the bodice over her head and made sure that it fit perfectly her curvaceous figure. Then she took the almost invisible strands of silk and sprinkled tiny, black onyx beads as minute as grains of pepper on the silk mesh, following the lines of her body, giving an air of provocative mystery.

When Ellen had seen the gown for the first time, she had gasped in utter disbelief at its beauty. Joy was completely satisfied with the finished project.

She had worn the gown only once. But once was enough. Atlanta socialites were still talking about it. When she had arrived at the Piedmont Driving Club with John, all eyes had turned in her direction. She could hear the "ooohs" and "aaahs" as she spoke to one friend and then another. Her reputation as a designer had been firmly established that night.

No, she would not take "The Painted Lady" gown with her to Boca Raton. It was not the kind of dress in which one dined alone. But she reveled in the happiness it had once brought to her. She was caressing the gown when her thoughts were interrupted by Ellen's cheerful voice, "Soup's on!"

Joy zipped the garment bag around the gown and joined her friend for supper.

After supper, Joy hugged the older woman impulsively. "I really don't know what I would do without you, Ellen," she said. "Sometimes I miss Mother and Daddy so horribly. It seems that, when they left, they took all the brightness out of my life—all, that is, except for you."

Ellen reached over and patted Joy's hand.

"As they used to tell me," Joy sighed. "Christians shouldn't accumulate their treasures on this earth. Well, I have been richly blessed with material things—but my *real* treasures are surely in heaven now."

Ellen sighed. "Joy, dear, Townsend and Faire would be the last to want you to feel that their love was your only real treasure. Pardon an old lady's preachments, but I think Jesus was talking about His love and the deep joy that one finds in Him whatever the circumstances. I happen to know that you were named for that eternal kind of love—your parents' most priceless possession."

"Oh, Ellen!" Joy choked back the sobs. "Will I ever really feel it again? I know God's promises are true—that only His grace is sufficient—not beautiful gowns, or charming cottages, or even dear friends like you—but He seems so distant, so remote. There is an empty place in my heart—as if it had no home. I'm afraid, Ellen, that right now my feelings don't match my name."

"Then it's fortunate, isn't it, that we don't have to rely on our feelings. Just keep believing, Joy. Just keep believing."

They sat for a moment in companionable silence—Ellen's worn Bible open to her favorite passage—and read together the familiar words that had sustained her through her widowhood and the death of two infant children: "Come to me, all you who are weary and burdened, and I will give you rest. Take my yoke upon you and learn from me; for I am gentle and humble in heart: and you will find rest for your souls."

Before Joy went to sleep, Ellen slipped the Bible into an open suitcase, beneath the scented tissue. It seemed only right that Joy should carry with her this divine Love Letter as she was setting out to put back together the slivers of her broken world.

Morning dawned bright and clear. Both women had slept well and felt refreshed. They ate a quick breakfast and tended to some last-minute details before leaving for the airport. Joy checked the contents of her suitcase, adding her make-up kit. Ellen made up the sofa bed, placed Granny's wicker bed in the Mustang, and carried along some extra cans of cat food. She would drop Joy off at the terminal on her way to The Boutique.

The cat remained unruffled throughout the proceedings; she was as much at home in Ellen's apartment as she was in her own cottage. Granny was then put in her bed on the back seat of the car, the luggage was stowed in the trunk, and Ellen and Joy climbed into the Mustang.

There was a minimum of confusion at the busy Atlanta airport as Ellen drove up to the loading zone. The porters were quick to unload the luggage and check Joy's tickets. Joy hugged her friend, patted Granny, and entered the sliding-glass doors opening into the noisy terminal.

Ellen watched her walk away. *Please, dear Lord, help Joy find You again. She feels so lost and lonely. Show her that she is always surrounded by Your love. And, Lord, please bring back that joyful spirit. I miss the happy girl I knew . . .''*

Her whispered prayer was interrupted by the honking of horns as other passengers rushed to catch planes. Granny whimpered. Ellen accelerated the sporty little car and shot out into the flowing traffic leading from the airport.

CHAPTER 3

THE WARMTH OF THE Florida sunshine and the soft sea breeze performed their magic to produce a slightly more relaxed expression on Joy's face as she waited for the driver to put her luggage into the limousine. She stood facing the breeze, closed her eyes, and breathed deeply.

The beautifully tailored mohair coat that had only hours before felt perfectly comfortable in the brisk air of early-morning Atlanta was now entirely too warm. As she removed the coat, she smoothed the skirt of her teal blue dress. Her shoulder-length hair, dark honey-blond with highlights of pale wheat, glistened in the sun. Even here in Palm Beach where the "beautiful people" congregated, she was striking. To the casual observer, she appeared to be a self-assured and confident young woman. Nothing could have been further from the truth.

Inclement weather at the point of origin had delayed the plane's departure from Hartsfield International, and she had arrived two hours later than anticipated. She was eager to get to the Boca Raton Hotel and Club for a much-needed respite from her problems. She felt they were becoming almost insurmountable. Surely two weeks of solitude in this tropical setting would help her put things into perspective, and she could again function as a happy and productive woman.

Glancing once more at the driver, she realized that he was loading some rich leather luggage into the limo beside hers. It had a distinctly masculine look. The last thing she needed now was to share the ride to the hotel, especially with a man. As far as she was concerned, she wanted to have as little contact with men as possible. Her recent broken engagement to John was still as painful as an open wound. All she wanted now was solitude.

"If I'm riding with *you*, then this trip has definite possibilities." The man's voice startled her.

Turning abruptly, she found herself looking into brown eyes, flecked with gold. They were accentuated by heavy, dark eyebrows, and emphasized by tiny laugh lines creased in a friendly grin. For a long moment she took in no other detail of the man's appearance—just those eyes. Realizing that she was staring, she turned away as he said, "I'm Brett McCort, and you are . . . ?"

Her rotten mood was no reason to forget her manners, she thought, but at this moment she wanted to rebel. She bit back a curt reply, and said, "Joy Lawrence."

"Well, Joy Lawrence, I'm looking forward to knowing you better."

"Don't count on it." Forget the good manners! She wanted to let him know that she needed neither conversation nor companionship. She just wanted to be alone. Why couldn't Greta Garbo have been riding with her instead. *She* would have understood.

Brett gave her a slightly crooked smile that appeared to be a challenge but said nothing. He turned toward her, studying the interesting planes of her face—the perfect symmetry of her features.

Joy sat stiffly erect and stared straight ahead as they pulled away from the airport and headed toward the interstate highway. Her life had crumbled in such a short time, she thought.

It had been only nine months since both of her parents had been killed in a tragic automobile accident on another interstate highway as they were returning home to Atlanta. Joy had been devastated. This tragedy combined with the death of her older brother, Bill, in Vietnam left her completely alone.

Memories ravaged her thoughts like a storm-tossed sea. The painful emotions they evoked were made bearable only because there had been so much love in the family. She recalled how Bill had teased her. "The day they brought you home from the hospital—a tiny, six-pound bundle wrapped in a soft-as-down blanket, Dad told me to climb up on the sofa and stretch out my arms. I was shaking so hard I almost gave you the colic, but you smiled up at me. Then Dad said, 'Billy, little Joy is yours to love and help care for.' It never occurred to me that there were nurses, maids, and two adoring parents looking out after both of us. You were always my private 'charge.' And you know what, sweetheart? I have never stopped feeling you're something very special!''

Now there was no other human being to whom Joy felt special—except, perhaps, to Ellen. When she had turned to John, her fiancé, for help in sorting out the tangle of legal problems arising from the probate of the wills, she had discovered how immature, unfeeling, and unreliable he really was. It was then that she had returned his ring and cancelled all plans for their wedding.

Startled from her reflections, she heard Brett say,

"Someone as beautiful as you shouldn't frown so much. Didn't your mother tell you that your face might freeze like that?"

She turned and with a tired little smile said, "I'm afraid my thoughts weren't happy ones. And I think my face has already frozen like this."

"Then I want to be around for the spring thaw! Anything a stranger could do to help a lady in distress?"

"Thank you, but I really came here to get away for a while. I—I just want to be alone." She didn't mean to be unkind, but the man was so persistent!

He was silent only a short time before beginning another line of questioning. "Are you from Atlanta?"

"Yes—Buckhead."

"Lovely place—I have an apartment near there . . . I'll bet your tyrannical boss sent you down on business, and you're fuming because you won't have time to hit the beaches!" He grinned in triumph.

The man wouldn't give up! "I don't have a boss," she responded coolly.

"Aha! Then *you're* the tyrannical boss—and you're regretting your decision to leave and let someone else mind the store."

"Wrong again!" This time Joy could not restrain a slight smile.

He threw up his hands. "I give up!"

The expression of dismay on his face was so appealing that Joy relented and told him a little more about herself. "I own a small boutique and design a line of clothes that is sold there."

"Ah, I should have known. You really know your colors. The dress you are wearing makes your eyes sparkle like aquamarines."

His approving look did not stop with her eyes, but

traveled down her trim figure, over her shapely legs and to her toes peeking from the sleek, sling-back sandals.

Joy tensed noticeably. She felt the color rush to her cheeks. His attitude was becoming entirely too personal. She turned and looked out the window, putting an end to further conversation.

Before she realized it they had turned onto El Camino Real. It was just as she had remembered. Some of the royal palms had been replaced, but a few remained near the circle. When she was a small girl, she had pretended that the tall palms lining the sides of the wide boulevard were giant soldiers standing at attention while she, the princess in her golden carriage, rode by, waving to the people she passed. How simple and uncomplicated those childhood days had been. Could anyone ever recapture that same happy feeling? How she wished it were possible!

Brett broke the silence. "A quarter for your thoughts."

"Has inflation raised the cost of thoughts *that* much?" Joy smiled in spite of herself.

"Only for special thoughts," he answered. "And anything that could bring a smile like that would be worth a quarter."

"I was just remembering some childhood fantasies I had when I vacationed here with my parents. I used to pretend that I was a princess in a golden carriage riding down this same street." She glanced at him hesitantly, hoping he wouldn't make fun of her.

His expression softened as he said, "I don't find it hard to picture you as a princess. In fact, you seem to fit the part quite well."

The limousine swung off the circle into the palm-lined main entrance to the Cloister. The exit and entrance drives were divided by a wide median, planted with exotic flowers so beautiful that one passing glimpse was never enough.

"Oh, there's Pan!" Joy exclaimed, her face alight with pleasure for the first time since the trip had begun.

Brett, pleased to see her happy expression, urged her to continue. "Who's Pan?" he asked.

"The statue there between the two sets of wrought-iron gates. Don't you know your Greek mythology?"

"No, but you could give me a brief lesson."

She was not sure whether he was teasing her, but she launched forth. "Pan was the god of pastures, forests, and flocks. Various stories are related to Pan. One of them tells that the nymph, Syrinx, fled from him and was transformed into a bed of reeds, whereupon Pan took reeds of unequal length and invented the shepherd's pipe. He challenged Apollo, god of music, to a musical contest. Apollo won and poor Pan had his ears changed to those of an ass for objecting to the decision. When Tiberius was the Roman emperor, it was said that passengers of a ship thought they heard a voice shouting that Pan was dead. The early Christians believed this story was a reference to Christ's birth and an indication that a new era was beginning."

"That's much more interesting than any history lesson I was ever taught," he commented sincerely. "With you as my teacher, chances are that I could improve my limited education."

"From the looks of things, you seem to be quite successful at whatever it is you do. So you must have more than a limited education." She allowed herself to eye him appraisingly.

"Well, I graduated from Auburn University with a degree in architecture, but I majored in football. To tell the truth, I just studied what was necessary to get my degree. Lately I have regretted not having read anything much but professional journals and an occasional Robert Ludlum thriller."

Engrossed in conversation, neither realized that the car had stopped and the uniformed doorman was opening the door for Joy. As she started to step out, she turned and gave Brett a goodbye smile.

"You can't get rid of me that easily," he grinned. "I'm staying right here at the Cloister. You thought I'd be staying at the Tower or the Beach Club, right?"

"Right," she admitted.

"Princess, you don't own the copyright on memories. My folks brought me here when I was a child, too, and I enjoy coming back whenever I'm in the area. And besides, when I get home, my mother will insist on knowing about all the changes and the interesting people I've met. You're the most interesting to date!"

He put his hand firmly on Joy's elbow and steered her through the doors into the spacious lobby. As she looked to her left and then to her right, she recognized the ornate ceilings, chandeliers, and arches of all descriptions that had brought world renown to the grand old hotel. A myriad of graceful fishtail palms, green plants, and colorful floral arrangements were a delight to the eyes. All of these and the lovely furnishings gathered from around the world combined to make a truly elegant entrance. It seemed to Joy that she had stepped back in time to the early part of the century. She felt very much at home. Her mother had probably been right when she had said that Joy belonged to 'an earlier time.'

Brett stood patiently watching as she took in every detail, trying to etch each of them indelibly into her mind. Reluctantly she moved toward the registration desk. The clerk smiled at her and told her that Peter, the bellman, would take care of her luggage and show her to her room. He also offered her some brochures that would help her find her way around the huge complex. She flipped through the booklets, admiring photographs of the twenty-six story Tower that loomed beside the Cloister and the Boca Beach Club, which had been built since her last visit.

While Peter was getting her room key from the desk clerk, she told Brett goodbye. Then she followed the pleasant young man who was carrying her luggage to the elevator. As she stepped into the elevator, she heard another bellman call to Peter to hold the door. Brett was following close behind, an impish look in his eye.

When they stopped at the third floor, she realized that he was getting off with her. Had he arranged this? Hadn't she tried to make it clear that she wanted to spend this time completely alone? The relaxed feeling she had begun to enjoy during the latter part of their ride was rapidly dissolving into irritation. She resolved to avoid further contact with him.

As she followed the bellman into her room, she heard Brett's voice call light-heartedly, "Princess, would you believe my room is just next door to yours?"

"Oh, no!" she groaned. Well, that was par for the course. Everything she had attempted lately had gone awry. Why should things change now?

Closing the door, she turned to savor the beauty of the room. Outside, amid all the tropical trees, stood the majestic, old Banyan tree, its leaves glistening in the sun. The rest of the room was just as she had remembered it, but with Brett next door, she felt that she would find it hard to relax. Why did he have to come here—and now—of all times?

Joy kicked off her shoes, slipped out of her dress, and donned an azalea-pink jump suit, trimmed with narrow bands of spring green. She walked to the window and looked at "her" Banyan tree and the golf course on which it stood. It seemed incredible that everything could be so green and spring-like here, when only a few short hours away by plane, the trees were bare, and snow and ice covered the ground. Oh, just to be able to relax in this beautiful place, with no schedules to meet, would be heavenly, she thought. She decided to stretch out on the bed to rest for just a few minutes. Then she would take advantage of that fabulous swimming pool.

The insistent ringing of the phone reached Joy's sleep-drugged brain, and she stirred. Where was she? The room was dark, and she was completely disoriented. At last her eyes became accustomed to the semi-darkness. She turned on the bedside lamp and reached for the phone.

"Hello," she murmured groggily.

"Hi, Joy. Are you ready for dinner?" Brett's voice sounded cheerful and expectant.

Joy grimaced. "I didn't know that we had any plans for dinner, and besides, you waked me!"

"Sorry about that. I bet the frown lines are very deep now. I can almost see them through the phone. But you do have to eat, don't you? I know you didn't have any lunch, because the flight was delayed. Come on now—smile just a little and tell me you will have dinner with me. Why should both of us eat alone?"

"Okay, okay," she quickly replied. She knew he would persist until she gave in. Maybe she could nip this little relationship in the bud before it got completely out of hand.

"Great! Can you be ready in about thirty minutes? And will the 'Court of Four Lions' be all right? It's quiet and casual there—the perfect place to unwind." His voice clearly showed his desire to please.

"Fine," she agreed. I'll be ready in half an hour." She stared at the telephone. If Brett hadn't asked her to dinner, she probably would have either skipped the meal entirely or just picked at her food. With all she had to accomplish in the next two weeks, she didn't need to miss any meals. She had already lost entirely too much weight. Not only were her clothes too large, but her face had become almost gaunt. Yes, she would have this one dinner with him, and then she could spend the rest of her visit alone, as she had intended.

After a quick shower, she went to the huge walk-in closet and looked around approvingly. What a pleasure it was to have room in which to hang an entire season's wardrobe without pushing and shoving hangers back and forth. At the end of the closet was a chest, large enough to accommodate everything from hats to shoes. Joy decided that, when she built a house, she would include a closet like this one. Glancing through her dresses and suits, she selected a ribbon knit skirt and a matching long-sleeved pullover with a flipped-up collar, scalloped along the edge. The hyacinth blue emphasized her eyes that now sparkled under long, curling lashes.

She reached into her small, brocade jewelry roll and lovingly removed an unusual gold locket which had belonged to her maternal grandmother. On the oval face was etched a single delicate rose. Each petal of the rose had been embedded with bits of "rose gold," which had been very popular in her grandmother's time. She opened the locket and studied pictures of her grandparents, looking very solemn, as was the custom for portraits in their day. She carefully fastened the clasp, letting the locket rest just in the curve between her firm, small breasts. The pale blue of her pullover sweater was the perfect backdrop for this treasured keepsake. Only small gold hoops at her ears were needed to complete her outfit.

She checked her make-up once more and ran a comb lightly through her softly waving, shoulder-length hair. Smiling at her reflection in the mirror, she was aware that

41

she already evidenced the refreshing sleep and change of scene. Her spirits lifted.

Promptly at eight-thirty there was a knock on her door. When she opened it and saw Brett standing there, she was startled by his rugged good looks. She had paid little attention to him during the ride from the airport. Now as he stood there smiling, her heart skipped a beat. Quickly she turned to reach for her clutch bag, hoping that her approving glance had not been too obvious.

Brett was the first to speak. "Well! You look as if the nap revived your sagging spirits."

"Yes. I can't remember when I've been able to take a five-hour nap. It was pure luxury," she replied, suddenly realizing that her sleep had been untroubled and—dreamless.

The restaurant was almost completely surrounded by windows overlooking the golf course, now dark and deserted for the day. Brett seemed to belong in a setting like this, she thought. Exposed wooden beams and a massive, but artistic, wooden lighting arrangement in the center gave the room a feeling of an English hunt club. The maitre d' pulled out a comfortable leather-covered chair for Joy as Brett seated himself to her right.

Joy glanced at him appreciatively, noting his neatly tailored navy blazer, pale blue shirt, and khaki slacks. His designer tie showed his excellent taste in clothes. But it was his tanned face, framed by the thick, wavy, dark hair—and his penetrating eyes—that would turn any woman's head.

When Brett asked if he might see a wine list, Joy murmured that Perrier water would be fine. The waiter took the order and departed.

"Well, Princess, we have one more thing in common. I

don't drink either. Guess it's because I really did try to stay in training when I played football at Auburn—or my strict upbringing. My conscience bothered me even if the coaches didn't know when I broke training,'' Brett confessed.

This was the second time Brett had mentioned his family, Joy observed. Strange how one's background continued to affect every experience of life—even into adulthood. Joy glanced down at the heavy pewter service plates and the usual seven pieces of flatware on the table in front of her. She remembered how her mother had taught her to start with the piece of silver that was on the outside and work toward the plate. It had been so simple after it was explained, but it had been an awesome decision for a small girl.

When the waiter returned with the Perrier water and had taken their dinner orders, Brett turned to Joy and said, ''You're smiling to yourself again.''

''Yes, I was just thinking what a powerful impression, either good or bad, parents can make on a small child. I was very fortunate to have had two who really cared. . . . Tell me about your family,'' she said quickly, before Brett could question her.

''My parents live in Atlanta. I have a brother, Scott, who is two years younger than I. He is connected with an insurance firm in Atlanta. My 'little sister,' Laura, is twenty-four and works for a television station there. None of the three of us is married. Mom and Dad think they will *never* have any grandchildren. Apparently they made home so pleasant for us that we all wanted to stay as long as possible. I moved out two years ago at the ripe old age of thirty and got an apartment closer to my office. But Scott and Laura show no signs of cutting the apron strings,'' he chuckled.

''I can't help but envy you. It would be so wonderful to have a family like yours. You must have had some happy times together.''

Brett looked at her quizzically. He wasn't sure if he should ask about her family because such a wistful expression crossed her face when she mentioned them. But without asking, he would never know, so he plunged ahead, "And how about your family?"

Joy winced. It was still so hard to talk about them. "My only brother was killed in Vietnam and both of my parents died in an automobile accident nine months ago." Surely he would not probe further.

Brett watched as her eyes misted and the worry lines appeared once again on her forehead, and wisely refrained from further questions. He smiled sympathetically and said, "Well, I have enough family to spare. Why don't you share mine?"

He was trying so hard to make her feel better. She was touched.

"How do we work out the custody arrangement?" she asked. "Do I get your mom and dad or Scott and Laura?"

With the tension eased, he smiled. The creases that were almost elongated dimples on either side of his mouth deepened, and the laugh lines beside his eyes grew more pronounced. Joy wondered why she had never noticed the deep cleft in his chin. *He has a nice face*, she thought.

"This summer you will have to go with us to our house on Lake Allatoona. We always have a terrific time there. Do you water ski?" he asked.

"I can manage a short distance on two skis, but that's about all. I do like to swim and sail, though."

"With all the McCorts teaching you, it won't be long until you'll be ready for competition at Callaway Gardens," he assured her.

Joy's laughter bubbled forth at the absurd idea. She was startled. How long had it been since she had heard herself laugh?

Brett watched as Joy devoured the last bite of her shrimp, scallop, and mushroom kabobs. How could one small woman consume such enormous amounts of food? She had started her meal with steamed cherrystone clams, followed by soup with large pieces of pita bread that had been dipped in butter, sprinkled with garlic salt and parsley, and broiled lightly. Very little of the mound of spinach salad remained, and now she appeared to be thoroughly enjoying the last tidbit of artichoke with hollandaise sauce.

Brett looked at her now contented face and laughed heartily. "Young lady, I may just have to rent a golf cart to drive you back to your room. You surely can't walk after downing such a meal. And you still have room for *dessert*. Incredible!"

CHAPTER 4

SLOWLY, VERY SLOWLY, Joy opened her eyes. She yawned and stretched languidly, savoring every moment. How long had it been since she had been able to sleep as late as she wanted? Outside, the world was dewy-fresh.

Suddenly a brilliant flash of scarlet caught her eye. She jumped out of bed and rushed to the window. There, sitting on a branch almost close enough for her to touch, was a cardinal. His plumage, so unbelievably red, was in startling contrast to the shiny, dark green leaves of the tree. Joy watched him, entranced with the colors. Maybe, just maybe, she would sketch a dress this morning—emerald green silk with a mandarin collar, accented by vermillion red piping and frog closings—an Oriental design. Yes, that would be striking, she decided. The cardinal, sensing that he was being observed, darted away. Joy's breath caught in her throat. It was almost as if God had sent the bird as a harbinger of hope.

Her adrenalin had begun to flow. She showered quickly and donned a cornflower blue wrap skirt, appliqued with white eyelet butterflies and a matching tee top. She added just a touch of lipstick and blush to her already glowing face, then grabbed her sketch pad and shoulder bag, and hurried downstairs to breakfast.

She stepped off the elevator and rushed into the lobby. Quite a distance away she noticed a familiar figure. That couldn't be Brett! He had been immaculately dressed each time she had seen him, yet there he was wearing a bush jacket, khaki pants, and boots—of all things. Under one arm he was carrying rolls and rolls of paper that appeared to be blueprints. Strange, she thought. She had never asked him why he had come to Boca Raton. Where was he going? His appearance was so out of character with the elegance of the surroundings that she cringed as if she had just heard chalk scraped across a blackboard.

As Brett strode toward the glass entrance, he glanced over his shoulder and saw Joy staring at him in disbelief. His eyes crinkled as a slow smile formed on his lips. He turned and walked toward her.

"What's wrong, Joy? Did you think that I had turned into a 'rambling wreck from Georgia Tech'? I'm a War Eagle from Auburn, remember?" he teased, enjoying her noticeable attempt to mask her disapproval.

"Uh . . . uh . . ." Joy stuttered. "I'm sorry. Please forgive me. I hardly recognized you. You must admit you do look a little different in that outfit."

"These are my 'work clothes'," he explained.

"You told me you studied architecture," she said hesitantly. "I thought architects sat in offices and designed buildings and bridges and things like that?"

"Yes, ma'am, they do," he exaggerated his Southern drawl, "but they also have to see that those things are built the way they're designed. And it's mighty hard to climb over concrete blocks and piles of steel when you're wearing a three-piece suit and wing-tip shoes."

47

Joy blushed. Who was she to judge someone by appearances? She certainly had been taught never to do that. Yet she was guilty, and he had been aware of it. A wave of regret swept over her.

"Will you have dinner with me tonight?" he inquired.

In anticipation of just such a moment, Joy had carefully rehearsed all the things she would say to Brett that would discourage further overtures on his part. She had almost let herself become involved again, and that would have been a mistake. However, none of those tactful speeches came to mind now that she needed them.

After what seemed to be an interminable pause, she answered, "Brett, thank you, but I can't. As I told you, I came to Boca for one reason—to be alone and to sort out some personal problems. I really do need some time to be by myself."

His face clouded. "You don't want to be seen with such a disreputable character, right?"

"I didn't mean that at all. And I don't want to hurt your feelings. I told you the truth. I came here for solitude. If I can get to know myself, then I will have something to offer others. Honestly, since my world came apart, I'm not sure who I really am. I just need some time." She could see by his expression that he was offended. "Please believe me," she added.

"Okay, Joy, have it your way. But I don't give up easily. You can bet your last dollar on that!" He turned on his heel and stalked out the front door to his rented Grand Prix, parked under one of the porte-cocheres.

Joy watched the silver automobile until it disappeared. She trudged into the dining room. Her appetite had disappeared and the exuberance of a few moments before had turned into a gloomy, gray blob which engulfed her like a fog.

She pushed the golden brown pieces of French toast and crisp bacon around on her plate, her fork making random designs in the thick maple syrup. Joy was more convinced than ever that she should never become attached to anyone again, much less fall in love. All the important people in her life had either died, or she had been parted from them under unhappy circumstances. The pain of loss was not worth the risk. No question about it! She would just have to stay out of Brett's way. She had begun to like him and, if their relationship continued, one of them would surely get hurt.

Sketch pad in hand, Joy walked out the front entrance into the courtyard. Flowers bloomed in such dazzling profusion that her eyes were unable to absorb their brilliance. The riotous color was a shock to her entire system. She needed peace and tranquillity.

Then she remembered the Banyan tree. That was the perfect spot. As she walked through the courtyard and around the side of the building, she passed a couple strolling hand-in-hand on the pathway. A radiant girl gazed back at the Cloister, enraptured with its grandeur. "I love the color of the hotel. What shade would you call it? Conch-shell pink? No, that's too coral. I know, Picasso pink. That's it," she babbled excitedly. "It is just the shade of pink Picasso would use in one of his paintings. And the red-tiled roof is just perfect. No Spanish-style building would be complete without real red tiles."

Her companion nodded. "The hotel would be right at home on the Mediterranean coast, among all of those old villas. Are you really happy that we came here for our honeymoon—instead of taking the Caribbean cruise?"

The girl smiled up into his face, "Of course, I'm happy! I feel as if I've stepped back in time—as if I were in Spain itself. But I would be happy anywhere with you."

Joy watched as the young man put his arm around his new

wife's waist. Slowly they walked away, caught up in their own special feelings. It must be wonderful, she mused, to love someone as much as that young couple apparently loved each other. She shook her head trying to clear her thoughts. *Stop it, Joy! This tropical setting has gone to your head. Get on with your business. And your business is not a romantic adventure. It is dress designing and resting your brain!*

The honeymoon couple's conversation had rekindled her interest in the Cloister. She was aware that most old Spanish buildings were entered through a courtyard; this was no exception. Turning slowly, she looked at the pair of L-shaped wings that extended from each end of the main part of the building and almost surrounded the courtyard. Only the gatehouse where Pan stood playing the pipes and two sets of wrought-iron gates were needed to complete the enclosure.

Joy walked to the center of the courtyard and sat on one of the colorful tile benches that faced the magnificent fountain. She knew that Ponce de Leon had come to Florida presumably to find the "Fountain of Youth." Though he had failed, perhaps she could find the Fountain of Life—a renewal of heart and purpose that seemed to elude her grasp.

In the center of the fountain was a statue of a lightly draped woman standing on a round pedestal supported by tall columns. Wasn't she called the "Lady of Boca"? Joy tried to remember. Looking upward, she saw that the woman's mouth turned upward slightly, almost in a Mona Lisa smile, and she held her head high and proud. Joy wondered just what the model had been thinking when she posed for the sculptor to fashion this extraordinary figure. She must have had a secret that even the artist could not guess. Near the base of the fountain, water spurted from the mouth of gargoyles. The decorative tiles which lined the base seemed to glow as brightly as the tropical blossoms. And all around Joy were citrus trees laden with their golden fruit, just begging to be plucked.

Then she glanced up at the front of the magnificent hotel. Twin towers rose on either end, and windows of all sizes and shapes added softness to the pink facade. Soaring arches made of coral rock and draped with cerise bougainvillea formed double porte-cocheres at the front entrance. Yes, Joy thought, this sight would charm even the weariest traveler.

She strolled through the open gates and turned to follow the pathway that paralleled the wing of the building. Just ahead lay one of the golf courses. Its greens were lush and velvety. The sand traps looked like bowls of sugar with several scoops removed. And the colorful, sometimes outlandish, attire of the many golfers was the only thing marring the verdant ribbon stretching into the distance.

I wonder if Brett plays golf, Joy thought. What made him slip into her thoughts again? She scolded herself. She must stop thinking about him. There were more important matters to resolve without complicating things. Hadn't she just gotten out of one unhappy love affair? She definitely didn't need to plunge headlong into another.

Jogging her thoughts back to her surroundings, she noticed all the exotic trees and plants near the walkway. Pausing to read the plaques identifying the trees, she noted the giant bamboo from Ceylon, a monkey puzzle tree from Australia, a shaving brush tree from South America, a date palm from Arabia, and a lady palm from central Asia. *This is almost a United Nations of trees and plants,* Joy mused. Resolving to come back another time to enjoy the rare shrubs and flowers, she walked resolutely toward the huge Banyan tree.

This tree had fascinated her for such a long time. She

remembered her father telling her, "In India the Banyan trees grow to well over one-thousand feet around and up to eighty-five feet tall. Those long strands hanging down are aerial roots that grow to the earth. They give additional support to the evergreen tree as it grows larger in circumference, since the main trunk would not be able to support such a massive top."

This tree might not be as large as the ones her father had described, but it was very special to Joy. It was strong and sturdy. Heavy winds might break a few branches, but the tree staunchly survived. And the roots reaching down from the branches reminded her of a strong arm stretching to comfort a child. Its large, leathery leaves shed the rain and provided refuge in a storm.

Then she remembered that her father had also said, "This indomitable old tree has some of man's best characteristics. When you are a young lady, you should keep the message of the tree foremost in your mind. It will guide you in choosing your husband, my child." Then he had chuckled softly.

How strange, Joy thought. Daddy had compared this tree to a man. She was beginning to understand what he had meant. It was the reason she loved this old tree. The tree possessed the same qualities she admired in a man: sturdiness, strength, support, protection, compassion, and unbending faith. The frown lines appeared in her forehead. Did such a man exist?

She sat down on a bench, took her artist's pencil and began a sketch of the dress that she had pictured so clearly earlier in the morning. It refused to come to life. The difficulty in transferring her thoughts to paper still plagued her.

Tossing her materials aside, she walked over to the tree, lowered herself slowly to the grass, and leaned back against its huge trunk. The soft, green canopy formed by the tree's branches gave her a feeling of peaceful seclusion. She felt isolated from all of the noise and activity of other guests nearby. She struggled to relax. Her problems had not disappeared, but for the present she would try to enjoy this unique hideaway. She longed for a short interlude of inner calm.

The water in the pool looked particularly inviting that afternoon. Selecting a lounge chair slightly removed from the other sunbathers, Joy removed the skirt that matched her maillot. Her swimsuit, in watercolor stripes of aqua, blue, and lavender, accentuated her trim figure. Not wanting to wait a minute longer to feel the soothing coolness of the water on her skin, she walked to the diving board, paused for a moment, then plunged into the pool. She swam the full length without surfacing. Reveling in the sensation of the cool water, she swam lap after lap until she was exhausted.

Lifting herself to sit on the side of the pool, Joy gasped, trying to catch her breath after the strenuous exertion. She was definitely out of shape and would have to gradually work up to that kind of pace. As she watched the other swimmers, she heard a familiar voice. Turning around, she noticed an attractive dark-haired woman sitting just behind her.

"Joy, is that really you?" the young woman squealed.

Recognizing a friend from Atlanta, Joy exclaimed, "Marianna, how wonderful to see you here!" She rose quickly, hurried over to her friend, and kissed her lightly on the cheek.

"Do we have to come all the way to Florida to get together? It's been months! What have you been doing with yourself?" Marianna McAlister bubbled.

Joy dropped into a chair beside her and smiled at her exuberant friend. "I really am sorry that I haven't called you. So many things happened all at once that I had little time to keep in touch with my friends."

"I know it's been dreadful since you lost your parents. But tell me about the wedding. When are you and John getting married?"

Joy's face clouded as she answered, "The wedding's off. I gave John his ring back and cancelled all the wedding plans. But it's for the best. Our marriage would never have worked."

Marianna's voice reflected the pain she saw in Joy's eyes. "I'm so sorry. This has been a difficult year for you. But, Joy, I can't honestly say I'm sorry that you aren't marrying John. He gave Dan and me an uncomfortable feeling when we were with him. He apparently didn't like any of your friends, from what I hear."

"I'm afraid you're right. Unfortunately I didn't realize that until later. We were spending less and less time with my friends and more with the people who could help him climb the social and professional ladder."

"How sad," Marianna sympathized.

"Even sadder is the fact that John didn't mind using others to get there. I was one of those people. Our value systems were at complete odds. Isn't it strange that you can't see those things when they are happening to you?" Joy sighed and frowned slightly.

"But what finally brought you to your senses?"

"Well, after Mother and Dad died, Mother's boutique was dropped in my lap, and I had to make all the decisions about running it. Trying to get all of the legal problems concerning the wills and property straightened out kept me so busy that I could hardly breathe. But John expected me to continue to attend every social function with him as if

54

nothing had happened. His wishes and needs always came first. I'm just very glad I found out how insensitive he is before we were married," Joy confided.

Marianna nodded. "Honey, don't you worry. There are a lot of nice men out there who would jump at the chance to make you happy."

"I don't need that just now. All I need is time to get my world back together. It's in as many pieces as Humpty Dumpty after his fall. That's why I came down here—to try to put things in perspective. But enough about me. What have you been up to these days?" Joy asked.

Marianna laughed. "Oh, the usual glamorous routine of the ordinary housewife and mother—washing diapers, chasing a toddler, cleaning house, cooking . . ."

"I envy you," Joy stated truthfully.

"You're kidding me!" Marianna looked incredulous. "You have your designing. You travel to exciting places to buy the latest fashions for the boutique. You lead a really exciting life. And with your looks, you couldn't possibly envy *me*."

"You just may be one of the luckiest women alive, Marianna. Dan thinks you are the most wonderful wife in the world. He would do anything to make you happy. And Amy is a healthy, adorable little cherub. You have a lovely home. You are surrounded by love and security. You have everything that is really important. Don't you know that?" Joy asked pointedly.

"Yes, I suppose so. I know Dan loves me and Amy is so precious. Sometimes, though, I feel that my mental capacity is limited to bedtime stories, and my working skills are one level above scrubbing floors," Marianna smiled. "All of us 'nonworking' mothers are barraged from all sides about getting out and 'living up to our potential.' We tend to have terrible guilt complexes."

"What you are doing is just as important as what any so-called working woman is doing, maybe even more important. You can be sure Amy will profit from the time you are spending with her. And just think of all the things you do to make Dan happy. You are always there to support him. Your job doesn't conflict with his. Taking care of those you love certainly has to be an important career . . . Speaking of Dan, is he here with you?" Joy asked.

"Yes, he had to come down on business, so we left Amy with Grandma and took a few days off. But he has business meetings all day, so you and I will have to get together and catch up on old times. How would you like to have lunch with me tomorrow? Maybe we could go shopping at Royal Palm Plaza later."

Joy knew that a few hours with this relaxed and uncomplicated friend would be good for her. "Perfect! Where shall we meet—and when?"

"Will noon at the east end of the lobby be all right?"

"It will suit me fine. See you then." Joy smiled at Marianna and turned to retrieve her cover-up and beach bag before starting to her room. It had been good to see Marianna again. She had been one of her best friends for years. They had been college roommates, and Joy had been a bridesmaid in Marianna and Dan's wedding. She had missed her friends. Well, that was one problem she could begin to remedy right away.

Hoping to avoid seeing Brett, Joy ordered room service that evening. Almost before she had time to slip on a caftan, there was a knock at the door and a waiter appeared. Room service at the Cloister had always been prompt. The food was not only good, but it was served with a flair rarely found in today's fast-paced society.

Joy sat down to the linen-covered table and studied the one perfect pink rose in a crystal vase. The china and silver were arranged as if for a formal dinner in someone's home. These were the things she had remembered and loved about the Cloister. The management and staff had maintained the traditional formality she enjoyed so much. It gave guests the feeling that they were *dining,* not merely *eating.*

After a leisurely meal, Joy picked up a book she had purchased at the airport before she left Atlanta. Propping herself up in bed, she began to read. She had read only a few pages when the phone rang. Wishing that she could just ignore it, she let it ring several times. Perhaps there was an emergency at the shoppe. She picked it up reluctantly.

"Are you hiding from me?" Brett's voice was playful.

"Oh, it's you," Joy said with slight annoyance.

"Who were you expecting—Robert Redford?" he laughed.

"Frankly, I was hoping I wouldn't hear from anyone. I was just enjoying a quiet evening in my room."

"So . . . you ARE going to become a hermit while you are here."

Joy sighed, "No, not really, but I do want to have some time alone. Why should that bother you?"

"It bothers me because *you* bother me, that's why. I told you this morning that I don't give up very easily when I know what I want," Brett stated emphatically.

"You are one of those people who will do anything to get what he wants, regardless of whom he hurts, aren't you? Well, I've just had one unhappy experience with that kind of man, and I have no desire to become entangled again." Joy's voice held an edge of uncharacteristic harshness.

"Hold it just a minute! I think you misunderstood me. The last thing I want to do is to hurt you. You are the kind of woman I would do anything to *please*. What I meant was that you are a very attractive and desirable woman, and I'd like to have a chance to get to know you better. I don't intend to beat down that wall you have built around yourself. But I would like very much to persuade you to open the door. Maybe we could be friends, at least," Brett said.

"All right, so I misjudged you. Maybe I'm a little on the defensive when it comes to men right now . . . By the way, how did your work go today?" Joy asked, wanting to change the subject.

"Oh, pretty good. In the condo we're building south of Deerfield Beach, there are some materials that don't come up to 'specs' and those will have to be replaced. That always slows down the entire project."

Joy interrupted, " 'Specs?' "

"Oh, that's just slang for 'specifications.' You see, there are pages and pages of them that describe the type and quality of all materials we have specified to be used in building the condominium. I work with the engineers and contractor in checking to be sure that everything is up to par. Inferior quality in either workmanship or materials could cause big problems later. A group of local engineers is helping to supervise the construction. Frank and Sam have been a big help in bringing me up-to-date," Brett continued.

"I assumed you had been working on this building from the beginning."

"No, this is a new project for me. One of my partners, Pete Jennings, was originally assigned to the job, but he reinjured a knee that had been hurt when he played football. So he's in the hospital, and I'm filling in until he's up and around again," he explained.

"That's too bad," Joy murmured. "How long will he be in the hospital?"

"Nobody knows. It just depends on how fast he mends.

So my plans are very indefinite," Brett replied. "Tomorrow we hope to get things moving again. Every day lost is very costly, especially with current prices. But enough about me. When do you think you will be setting your foot out the door so that I can see you again?" he asked.

"I met an old friend from home at the pool today, and we plan to have lunch together tomorrow," Joy said, hoping to erase the "hermit" image from his mind.

"So, you can go out with other men, but I'm a 'no-no.' Is that how it is?" His voice held a cutting edge.

Joy tried to stifle a slight chuckle. "As a matter of fact, the friend is a lady—my college roommate. We haven't seen each other for quite a while. She asked me to have lunch with her, and then we plan to go shopping."

"Good. Just so long as it isn't with a long-lost lover," he stated firmly. "I would be jealous, you know."

She laughed again. "You're impossible. You hardly know me."

"Joy, time is irrelevant when you see someone very special. I just want you to know I'm staking my claim on you *now*."

Her voice grew serious. "Brett, please don't rush me."

"Okay, but I want you to know that I'm waiting, not very patiently, but I'm waiting. Have a good day tomorrow and I'll be in touch."

"Thanks . . . and good night," Joy replied and replaced the phone. She had enjoyed talking with him. There was something about him that attracted her like a sliver of steel to a magnet—even against her will. She would have to keep a tight rein on her feelings.

She picked up the book once more and tried to concentrate. The characters had already become jumbled in her mind, and she was forced to reread several pages to refresh her memory. Only a few moments later the book dropped from her hand as her body jerked involuntarily in the first stages of sleep. She roused enough to put the book on the bedside table and to turn off the lamp. She snuggled down into the warm, comfortable bed and almost instantly she was sleeping peacefully.

CHAPTER 5

YESTERDAY'S SUN HAD brought a healthy glow to Joy's cheeks, she noted with satisfaction as she glanced into the mirror. And today she had chosen one of her favorite dresses to wear to lunch. The wood block print of seashells showed coral against white on the overblouse, and reversed to white on coral in the cluster-pleated skirt. The silky polyester fabric caressed her legs when she walked. It was one of those dresses that made her feel especially good whenever she wore it.

Joy walked jauntily through the lobby. She stopped when she spotted the bell captain at the desk beside the entrance. "Domenick, it's so good to see you," she said happily as she walked toward him.

The man's face broke into a warm smile of recognition. "Miss Lawrence, it is good to have you back with us!"

They shook hands enthusiastically as Joy spoke. "However did you manage to remember my name after six years?"

"Miss Lawrence, it's good to have you back with us!" children. It's always good to see how much they grow between visits. But you have only grown more beautiful. I remember, when you visited with us, you would come down almost every day to get a bike and go for a ride.'' Domenick's soft voice brought back a flood of memories.

"I surely did,'' she recalled. ''You've seen so many of us kids grow up and come back, haven't you?''

"In thirty years, I am now seeing many of those children bringing their little ones back.'' His eyes sparkled as he spoke.

"Well, I have no children, but I hope you will be here when I *do*! I'm meeting a friend for lunch now, but I'll see you again before I leave.''

"Stop by, and I'll have a bike for you,'' he promised.

"I haven't ridden in years. You might have to use some first aid if I tried.''

They both laughed at her joke as she turned away and walked toward the end of the lobby. Joy thought that, for Domenick, it must be almost like a family reunion when he welcomed former guests after several years' absence. He was a precious link with the past.

Joy settled herself in one of the chairs and admired the Mediterranean furniture. Much of it had been imported from Europe when Addison Mizner built the Cloister in the 1920's. He certainly had left his imprint on this part of the state, she thought. He had even created Worth Avenue in Palm Beach, using the same Spanish-inspired style. The arches and tiles were just as prevalent in Palm Beach as here in Boca.

She glanced at her watch for the third time. Joy was always prompt. In fact, she often arrived well ahead of an appointment so that she would not keep anyone waiting.

Marianna, her dark hair waving softly around her pert face, walked rapidly across the lobby. She was a very attractive woman, Joy thought. Her gray-green eyes sparkled when she talked, and her face was constantly changing to reflect her mood or the feelings of those around her. She was wearing a smart vanilla suit with a jade green blouse. As Joy watched her approach, she decided that Marianna was certainly anything *but* the uninteresting housewife she had described.

"You knew, of course, that I would be late, didn't you?" Marianna's face was transformed by her happy smile.

"That thought had crossed my mind, but people do change, you know. I didn't want to take a chance just in case you had."

"Nope, not me. If I ever showed up on time, everyone would fall over in a dead faint!"

Both of them laughed heartily, remembering all the times that Joy had waited for her friend during the years they had known each other. It was good to be together again after such a long time. And to discover that some things *never* change—a reassuring thought.

Because neither of the women was very hungry, they took the limousine to the Royal Palm Plaza for a sandwich at the ice cream parlor. From the window of the plush automobile, Joy noticed that several changes had been made since her last visit. Suddenly her breath caught in her throat as the vehicle pulled to a stop at a traffic light. There, across the street in front of a coffee shop, was Brett! He was listening intently as a striking blonde talked animatedly. *Who is she?* Joy wondered. Brett McCort certainly did get around, didn't he? Oh well, why let a man spoil her day? She would forget all about him, she resolved, but was grateful when the limo made a right turn, obscuring her view of the attractive couple.

When Joy and Marianna entered the ice cream parlor, the hostess seated them at a small table next to the large front window which afforded them a view of part of the plaza and the shoppers as they passed. As this was the peak of the tourist season in South Florida, the small restaurant was filled to capacity. People of all ages, in a holiday mood, were sating their hunger. Joy was amazed at the number of children. She had expected to see mostly retirees.

"Where do you want to go when we finish eating?" Joy asked.

"You know me—wife and mother first. I'd like to do some shopping for Amy. She is growing out of her clothes as fast as I can buy them. Oh, but if that would be boring for you . . ." Marianna paused, her smooth brow furrowed with concern, "we could do something else."

"No, really, I would enjoy browsing in a children's shop for a change. Let's get a pamphlet that shows the location of all the stores, and we'll find one for children," Joy suggested.

The hostess was happy to provide a directory and, while they ate, the two young women pondered the directions to the more than eighty-five shops, restaurants, and offices in the "Pink Plaza."

"Aren't the names of the shops delightful!" Marianna exclaimed. "Listen to these: "The Gazebo, Snappy Turtle, The Tree House, Cricket Shop, and, how about this one, The Pink Pony! Wouldn't you just love to check them all out?" Shaking her head, she concluded, "It would take us a week to do this place justice. I had no idea it was so large. But if we don't get started, we'll never even make a dent!"

After finishing lunch they walked out into the warm sunshine. Clusters of buildings, all designed in the same unique style as the Cloister, surrounded them. The pink buildings, arched walkways, red-tiled roofs, and landscaping were as magnificent as that at the hotel. Bougainvillea, with its bright fuchsia flowers, draped over arches and walkways. Many different varieties of palms dotted the courtyards and gardens adjacent to the buildings. Wrought-iron grillwork added a decorative effect to the stairways and entrances. Fountains abounded in the gardens. Hibiscus, oleanders, poinsettias, snapdragons, and calendulas splashed their colors lavishly on the canvas of green and pink.

Eventually they located a children's store, and as Marianna shopped for Amy, Joy examined the tiny baby dresses. She picked up one and held the soft fabric to her cheek, allowing her thoughts to wander. She had always loved children and had even played with her dolls until she was well past the age when most little girls discarded them. With a deep, almost despairing sigh, Joy folded the tiny garment and put it back on the counter. *Enough wishful thinking,* she told herself. *Babies have to have fathers, and I don't plan to get married any time soon.* She turned away to inspect the appliqued pillows.

"Come see what I've found for Amy," Marianna called. "These should keep her clothed for a few months. The way she's growing, she'll be into another size soon. She's a real McAlister, like her daddy, but she is growing *up* and he is growing in another direction," she laughed. "Where do we go now?"

Joy thought for a moment, then answered, "There is a gift shop I particularly like—the Chambered Nautilus. Would you like to look around there?"

"Oh, yes! It would be heavenly to browse through china and crystal without having Amy's little hands reaching for everything in sight."

The seventeen buildings of the Plaza were all sizes and shapes. Some were set at angles to the others so that even the unusual-shaped spaces formed between them provided areas of cultivation for lush foliage and fragrant blossoms. The two women stopped several times and checked the little map to make sure they were headed in the right direction.

They emerged from one of the triangular gardens into a very large area that was almost like a small park. There, in the corner of one of the buildings, was the gift shop. Marianna looked at the name of the store and paused.

"I know this is a stupid question, but what is a chambered nautilus? It sounds like something from thousands of leagues under the sea!"

Joy grinned. "Don't worry, I had to ask, too. It's the name of a mollusk with a coiled and partitioned shell, lined with a pearly layer. That's a sketch of one." She pointed to the sign over the store.

As they entered, they were warmly greeted by a lovely, dark-haired woman who introduced herself as Mrs. Josephs and told them to feel free to browse as long as they wished. Marianna gravitated to the porcelain. She carefully examined an unglazed, perfect replica of a magnolia blossom made by Lefton. She was entranced by its beauty. The single delicate bloom would add the special touch she needed on her hand-carved mahogany table, and would be right at home in Atlanta, she decided.

Then Marianna noticed a highly glazed Capodimonte bowl filled with exquisitely realistic flowers. There were anemones, lavender-blue cup flowers, full-blown roses in shades of pink and yellow, and exquisite white daffodils with yellow throats and a touch of orange outlining the trumpets. She could just picture the bowl of porcelain flowers in the center of her dining room table. She picked it up and carried it to the smiling lady who had greeted them.

"I'm going to start a family heirloom myself," she said, "like those that have been handed down to me." While Marianna's purchases were being carefully wrapped and boxed, she wandered into another area of the store.

Meanwhile Joy had been standing in a room displaying every kind of Oriental treasure imaginable. Her gaze fell on an exquisite ming tree. It was breathtaking! The gnarled trunk and branches were shaped from fine strands of metal that had been twisted into a replica of an ancient, windblown tree. The leaves appeared to be coated with a dusting of priceless jewels. Perry Marshall had guided the skilled enamelists from Bovano in fusing glass crystals to copper, using the ancient techniques of cloisonné enameling. *Oh!* Joy thought. *Wouldn't I just love to have that piece in my home?*

Reluctantly she turned her attention to the other items— delicate, handpainted fans and embroidered wall hangings. She knew that one who had never done handwork could not possibly appreciate the time and patience required to create such works of art. Again Joy was grateful for her heritage —a family who encouraged learning such skills and creating things of beauty.

She was remembering how her grandmother had first taught her to embroider when she caught a glimpse of a display of handcrafted objects from China. There were elegant birds with enameled, filigreed wings. But before she could inspect them further, she noticed a vase nestled in a silk-lined, silk-covered box. It appeared to have been made from a gossamer web, spun from delicate strands of sterling silver. The vase was magnificent, she thought, but it was the card beside it that intrigued Joy. The message on the card read: *Cherry blossom. Offering the strength to endure the winter, the cherry blossom reveals beauty and warmth even at the worst of times.*

Joy turned to Mrs. Josephs and asked, "Where did you manage to find these indescribable treasures?"

A happy smile lighted the shop owner's face as she replied, "Oh, you like my favorites! This is an exclusive SuHai collection done by the artisans of Chengtu, China. Each filigreed vase is handmade and is numbered in a limited edition series. I'm very pleased to have this collection. The designs are said to bestow on the owner harmony in life.''

"I must have that vase. This has been the 'winter of my life,' and the message of the cherry blossom speaks to my heart.''

Noticeably puzzled, Mrs. Josephs carefully packaged Joy's purchase. The striking young woman showed no trace of sadness. What could be hidden behind that lovely face that would disturb her so?

Joy walked back to look· at the ming tree once more before she left. Tomorrow she would have to try again to sketch the emerald green-and-red dress. Seeing these lovely things had fueled her resolve to try again.

After leaving the gift shop, Joy and Marianna wandered through several other stores, their eyes feasting on a banquet of unique items. Marianna suddenly remembered that she needed to buy a birthday card to send to her brother. They located a card shop and, while Marianna made her selection, Joy read some of the humorous cards that were becoming very popular. She discovered that she was chuckling to herself and called Marianna to share some of the fun. The two of them lost all track of time as they giggled like small girls over the clever verses.

"It has been a long time since I have had such fun!" Joy said.

"Do you realize what time it is?" Marianna asked in amazement, as she checked her watch. "Dan is probably already back at the hotel, wondering where I am!"

The two young women hurriedly collected their purchases and went to the place where the limousine would pick them up and take them back to the hotel. On the ride back they chatted excitedly about their afternoon outing. Joy's spirits had lifted considerably, and she felt more like herself than she had in many months.

As they entered the hotel, Marianna asked, "Why don't you have dinner with Dan and me tonight? He said he wanted to be sure to see you while you are here."

Joy was hesitant to accept the invitation, feeling that the couple probably would prefer to dine by themselves. But, at Marianna's insistence, Joy conceded that it would be much nicer to have dinner with friends than to spend a lonely evening. After arranging to meet at eight o'clock, the friends parted to go their separate ways.

A relaxing bubble bath would be much better than a quick shower to ease her tired feet and body, Joy decided. She turned on the tap and slowly added the bath crystals. Immediately the water was transformed into iridescent bubbles of rainbow colors, swirling about in ever-changing patterns. Joy longed for a fabric that would duplicate the kaleidoscopic exhibition.

She slid into the tub, trying not to disturb the b   es. They floated around her body as she lay in the soothing water, letting her mind flow in random patterns like the colors of the bubbles. The day had been so filled with beauty. She wished that she could infuse some of it into her brain to erase the darkness of the depression she had been experiencing. Things did seem a little brighter, though. Spending the afternoon with Marianna had helped a great deal. And having dinner with her friends would be like old times.

The water had cooled and the bubbles had vanished before Joy's reverie was broken. Hurriedly she reached for a thick, fluffy towel and rubbed her skin until it tingled. Wrapping a soft, fleecy robe closely around her, she walked into the bedroom.

It had been days since she had watched television or read

a paper, so she flipped on the set to a national news broadcast. Settling back in an easy chair, she watched as correspondents narrated tragedies, wars, investigations, and legislative happenings. *Good grief!* Joy thought. *Does the news always have to be bad? Isn't there something happy that deserves media coverage?*

Flipping the dial again, she discovered a channel that continuously broadcast a listing of the activities that were available to guests of the hotel—water skiing, aquaslimnastics, fashion shows, an historical hotel tour, scuba classes, sailing, fishing, golf, tennis, movies.

She glanced at her travel alarm clock, jumped up, and hurriedly began putting on her make-up. Where had the time gone? At least she had always made a habit of laying her clothes out ahead of time. The tissue silk crepe de Chine caressed her body as she slipped the dress over her shoulders. While she tied the soft bow at her neck she studied her reflection in the mirror. What had Brett said about her knowledge of color? Yes, she admitted, the azure blue of the dress did heighten the darker aquamarine of her eyes.

She stepped into strippy sandals and turned once more to the mirror to comb her hair. She was lucky, she thought, that her hair had just enough natural wave that it wasn't necessary to spend valuable time curling it. Usually she could shampoo it, blow it almost dry, and then comb it lightly until it fell into soft waves to her shoulders. She was glad now that she had decided to have the pale wheat highlights added. Her hair had turned much darker over the past year or so, and the lighter strands gave it the sun-streaked look of a teen-ager.

Could she really be twenty-six years old? She should be taking better care of her hair and skin, Joy thought. Now was the time to begin a regimen to delay premature age lines and extra pounds. *Well*, she thought, *while I'm trying to get my head straightened out, I might as well work on my body, too.*

With that resolution Joy picked up the clutch bag that matched her sandals and started for the door. At the last minute she turned, walked to the closet, and selected a soft woolen shawl, woven in shades of blue, turquoise, and lavender. She knew that, even in Florida, the nights could be cool, and she wanted to be ready for whatever the evening held.

CHAPTER 6

WHEN JOY ENTERED the elevator, the operator smiled at her approvingly as she requested the lobby level. Though the elevators were self-operating during certain hours when few people were using them, there was an operator on duty for peak times. This practice was another example of the ways in which the Cloister gave their guests a cherished feeling. Those push-buttons could not smile at you or tell you to have a nice evening as this kind man did when she exited.

Joy made her way across the long lobby which extended from the east wing to the west wing of the hotel. Dan and Marianna McAlister arrived at their meeting place only moments later. Dan stepped over to Joy and gave her a bear hug.

"You look like a million dollars, Joy," he said, as he held her at arm's length. "Tonight must be my lucky night. I'll be having dinner with the two most gorgeous women around."

All three of them laughed. When Marianna hugged her, too, Joy was struck by the fact that she had missed this warm, affectionate touching and hugging that had always been so much a part of her family life and with close friends. John had detested outward displays of emotion— another distinct difference between them. She had no need to grieve over him. Their broken engagement was one of the best things that could have happened to her. Suddenly Joy was *sure* of that, and she felt a heavy weight lifting from deep within.

Putting an arm around each of the women, Dan continued, "Both of you are too pretty to hide in some dark restaurant tonight. How does the Cathedral dining room suit you? Every man in the place will be looking at you and envying me."

Without waiting for an answer, he guided them toward the dining room. As they entered, Joy gave a soft gasp. "I never come here that I'm not overwhelmed with the elegance of this room," she said. "Usually, when you return to a place you remembered from childhood days, it seems smaller and not as impressive. But this is even *more* magnificent than I remembered."

For a moment they stood admiring the lavish decor. Two rows of the famed 14-karat gold-leaf columns supported arches that extended upward to an incredible height. The ornate ceiling had caused many a neck to swivel in wonder. Suspended from the soaring ceiling, immense but delicately lovely golden chandeliers illuminated the dining room. Miniature replicas of these hung along the side walls, shedding a soft light on the diners.

The maitre d' led them to a table near the dance floor and assisted the women into comfortable upholstered chairs. The table, covered with a white damask cloth, was set with service plates in the hotel's unique china, and formal place settings of silver and crystal. Joy remembered how very grown-up she had felt when she had been seated, as a ten-

73

year-old child, with her parents. She had the same feeling now.

One particular memory of that visit would always be vivid in her mind. Her father had been an excellent dancer, and she had always enjoyed watching him dance with her mother. But on that night her father had spoken with the orchestra leader and, when he returned to the table, he bowed, not to her mother, but to Joy! "Young lady, may I have this dance?" he had asked.

With the memory, she could almost feel the blush that had suffused her face that evening. "But, Daddy, I can't dance as well as Mother. I would embarrass you." She had glanced at her mother, who smiled her approval.

"You would never embarrass me, Joy," her father reassured her as he took her hand and led her to the ballroom floor. They reached the floor just as the other dancers stood applauding the last medley. The orchestra leader looked over at her father, smiled, and the strains of "Misty" flowed melodiously over the room. Her father took her hand and led her in a graceful step.

"Joy, I asked them to play that song because I always think of you when I hear it. I wanted it played for our first 'formal' dance together."

"But what is the name of the song, and why does it make you think of me?" the little girl had asked.

"It is sometimes hard to explain why a song reminds you of someone, but I'll try. My first glimpse of you in your mother's arms on the night you were born touched me so deeply that my eyes filled with tears, and I wasn't able to see you clearly. My heart was so full of love for both of you that I wanted to hold on to that moment forever. Later that night, when I got into the car to go home, the first song I heard on the radio was 'Misty.' Since then I've always thought of you when I hear that song—because I first saw

74

you through misty eyes of love. Perhaps you will under-stand when you are grown and have a child of your own.". Her father's eyes had glistened with tears once again as he smiled down at her.

Joy felt a bittersweet happiness. How she missed those two wonderful people. But they had given her beautiful memories and a love that would be with her forever.

"Joy, dear, you aren't crying, are you?" Marianna's concerned voice interrupted her reverie.

"Only a few happy tears," Joy insisted. "I was just thinking of the wonderful times I spent here with my parents."

"Just wanted to be sure you are all right." Marianna reached over and patted Joy's hand.

The waiter had returned with a cooler and a bottle of Perrier. He poured the sparkling mineral water into frosted glasses garnished with slices of lime. Joy sipped her drink slowly, and her face brightened.

"Dan, do you stay in touch with many of the guys we knew in high school?" she asked. "We ought to have a reunion. Everyone is literally scattered all over the world now."

Dan told her about several mutual friends whom he still saw occasionally in business and at social gatherings. Marianna added interesting little anecdotes as they talked. The friendly conversation brought back the closeness the three had once shared.

Suddenly Marianna put her hand to her mouth and gasped. "Dan! I almost forgot! I want to reach Mother on the phone before Amy goes to sleep. Nobody answered when I tried to call earlier. I just have to hear from Amy, or I won't sleep a wink tonight!"

Dan agreed that she would, indeed, be wakeful and, what's more, that she would probably keep *him* awake if she didn't ease her mind about the baby's welfare. He rose to help her from her chair.

"I'll be back in a few minutes. Excuse me, please," she said as she hurried from the dining room to the nearest telephone.

While Marianna was away, Dan and Joy talked animatedly about the past football season. She had always enjoyed football. Her big brother, Bill, and her father had taken her to Little League practice and games, where she had become quite knowledgeable about the sport. She missed those talks. None of the women she knew liked football. Dan laughed and admitted that, in college, the guys had agreed that she was the only girl they could talk to who knew the difference between a defensive tackle and a split end.

"The year you were voted Homecoming Queen must have gone down somewhere in the history of the school. It was the first time a Homecoming Queen ever *watched* the football game!" Dan laughed heartily.

Joy studied his face as they talked. He had a knack for putting others at ease. He was an attractive man with blue-gray eyes and well-groomed, auburn hair. His suntanned face, sprinkled with lines that could have been created only by smiling, would definitely be described as warm and pleasant. Marianna was a lucky woman. She would certainly never tire of seeing that happy face across the breakfast table every morning.

Suddenly his expression grew serious. "Joy, don't turn around just now, but there is a man to your right who is staring daggers through both of us. When you have a chance, glance in that direction and see if you know him."

It was not necessary to see him. She recognized the deep voice asking the waiter about the various entrées. It was Brett! But why would he sit there, glowering? If he had seen her, why didn't he come to the table and speak to her?

Marianna returned, smiling broadly. "Amy is just fine. I spoke with her and she said, 'Mama.' Mother says that she has been an angel."

Dan kissed her lightly on the forehead as he held her chair. He had scarcely taken his seat when he rose again, staring over Joy's shoulder. She turned her head to find Brett at her side. His mood apparently had changed abruptly. He was now smiling and jovial. He spoke to Joy, then extended his hand to Dan.

"Brett McCort," his voice exuded friendliness. What had caused such a change? Joy was puzzled.

With introductions out of the way, Dan asked Brett if he would care to join them for dinner. He failed to see the slight shake of Joy's head as she tried in vain to discourage Dan's invitation. Brett accepted quickly, excusing himself only long enough to make the arrangements with his waiter.

"I had no idea you knew him, Joy. Why do you suppose he was glaring at us? He seems like a nice-enough fellow, though."

"I met him on the limousine ride from the airport in Palm Beach, and I have no idea why he should be acting so strangely. But I'm still trying to decide why the name 'McCort' should sound so familiar to me. It has been bugging me ever since we met." Joy's face wrinkled in thought.

Before they could conclude the conversation, the waiter returned to set a place for Brett. Dan and Joy had delayed their first course while waiting for Marianna to make her call. Now the four of them crunched on the crispy treats from the relish tray, and Joy smiled in anticipation as the waiter placed a bowl of watercress soup in front of her.

"Joy may be small, but you won't believe what she can consume at one sitting," Brett teased.

Then he proceeded to tell the other couple everything that she had eaten the night they had arrived. He embellished the story, making it impossible for Marianna and Dan to eat because they were laughing so heartily.

"Don't think you can shame me into eating less tonight. I intend to enjoy every bite of every course," Joy said in mock defiance. "And I'm even going to have melon sherbet for dessert," she added as the others continued to chuckle.

The dinner conversation flowed in a lively vein. The men discovered that, among their common interests, was the fact that their offices were located in the same area of Atlanta. Not wanting to bore their companions, they refrained from too much talk about business. Brett's natural wit and Dan's carefree banter kept everyone in high spirits.

When they had finished their entrées, Brett turned to Joy. "It's a shame to let all of that good music go to waste. I'm not the best dancer in the world, but would you at least give me a chance?"

Joy smiled in agreement, and he led her to the dance floor. The rhythm of the soft music made it easy to follow Brett, who was a very good dancer despite his modest evaluation. She relaxed in his arms, and they moved gracefully across the shiny floor.

When the music stopped for a moment, Joy asked, "Why in the world were you glaring at Dan before you came over to our table? You made him feel very uncomfortable."

Brett hesitated a moment and then confessed, "Oh, just a fit of jealousy, you might say. You had told me the *old friend* you were meeting today was a woman. Well, when I came into the dining room and found you and Dan making such a cozy, little twosome, I 'saw red.' I hoped to make him uncomfortable enough so that he would make it a short evening. Then I planned to ask you to go for a walk with me. How was I to know he had a wife who just happened to be out of the room when I came in?''

Joy, strangely pleased, continued, ''How did you know she was his wife, or that he wasn't really my date?''

''For crying out loud, Joy! He kissed her when he helped her into her chair. Would your date kiss another woman right there in front of you?'' He looked at her as if he thought she were a little more than dense.

She giggled, ''I'm afraid I didn't notice that little clue, Sherlock.''

''Stick with me, Dr. Watson, and we can have some interesting adventures,'' he smiled and hugged her to him as they continued to dance.

The music of Van Smith and his orchestra was exceptional. The band leader was also the pianist of the group. Unlike many other orchestras that Joy had heard, these musicians seemed to truly enjoy what they were doing.

Mr. Smith smiled and nodded as the dancers moved past and occasionally talked with them as he played the piano. As he finished a medley of songs, Joy and Brett stood directly in front of the band, applauding appreciatively. Smith asked Joy if she had a favorite song. When she shook her head, Brett requested ''You Light Up My Life.'' The pianist smiled and began to play the lovely melody without benefit of sheet music. The rest of the orchestra followed as if they had carefully arranged scores before them.

Brett held Joy a little closer as they danced. A feeling of déja vu swept over her. Long ago she had experienced this same event, when she had danced to the music of a song requested for her by her father. She reacted with a slight shiver.

Brett moved back slightly so that he could look into Joy's astonishingly blue eyes. ''You do light up my life, you know. I thought of that song the first time I saw you. Your hair shone so brightly in the sunlight at the airport that it seemed to form a halo around your head. You are the angel I have been needing.''

Joy shivered again at his words. She felt anything but angelic. If he only knew her anguish. Tenderly Brett kissed her lightly on the forehead before escorting her back to their table.

Their dinner ended pleasantly, but not until Joy had finished the last bite of her melon sherbet. Merriment sparkled in Brett's eyes as he pointed to the empty crystal dessert dish.

He turned to the McAlisters and commented, ''What did I tell you? She can eat more than a farmer at harvest time. Her grocery bill must rival the national debt.''

Joy joined in the friendly banter. ''You should see what I can eat when I'm *really* hungry!'' she exclaimed. Laughter erupted once more.

No one was ready for the enjoyable evening to come to an end, but Dan needed an early start the following morning, hoping to wind up his business. He and Marianna excused themselves reluctantly. Brett assured them that he would see Joy safely to her room, and the couples parted in the lobby, with Joy promising Marianna that she would be in touch the following day.

Brett took Joy's hand and they started across the lobby. Suddenly he asked, ''Would your shawl keep you warm enough for a short walk in the courtyard?''

Trying to retain the carefree feeling of the evening, she turned to him and said in a teasing voice, ''I think a walk would be good for me. It will settle my dinner so that I'll have room for a midnight snack.''

They walked arm-in-arm out the front door. Lights played on the fountain and the exotic plants in the courtyard. The citrus trees lining the drive were studded with tiny, white, twinkling lights; and the heavy fruit might have been shining ornaments on a Christmas tree.

"I feel as if I were in another world," Joy whispered, "a world of enchantment."

"Perhaps you are," Brett acknowledged. "I only know that I want to be included in that world." Brett's eyes were probing hers—trying to read there her reaction.

"Please, Brett, don't. You don't know anything about me—nor, I, you." Joy was frightened. "I have so many problems that need to be resolved. Can't we just enjoy spending some time together without any serious involvement? There's no room in my life just now for you—or any other man."

"Sorry, Joy. I guess I came on too strong. But maybe we know each other better than you think." With difficulty he shifted the mood to a lighter vein. "I'm not sure, but I think the 'Lady of Boca' is keeping a secret about us."

They gazed up at the magnificent fountain in the center of the courtyard. The Lady smiled mysteriously.

CHAPTER 7

AT HOME, JOY was an early riser—not wishing to miss a single moment of any day. In Boca, after a few leisurely mornings in which she caught up with her rest, she was back into her well-ordered routine. Today she had dressed in a nautical outfit—white twill pants and a matching middy blouse, accented with navy blue braid and a brilliant red sailor tie. A brisk walk up El Camino Real had increased her growing appetite and had heightened the color in her cheeks. She was among the first to enter the dining room.

Her mouth watered as she stared at the stack of luscious, golden pancakes. The butter melted and mingled with the raspberry syrup to form small rivulets which flowed across her plate toward the strips of crisp, lean bacon. She savored every delectable morsel. With a satisfied sigh she leaned back in her chair and sipped her second cup of coffee.

Brett's arrival in the dining room surprised her for some reason, though she had grown accustomed to his casual attire and the ever-present boots that he wore to work. When he spied her sitting alone, he approached her table.

"So, you ate all of the evidence before I could log the calories, didn't you?" His dark eyes twinkled merrily as he spoke.

"Why do you think I got up at the crack of dawn?" Joy replied in mock indignation. "I need all of my strength today because I plan to get to work."

"I'll let you off the hook this time. But if I promise not to ask what you ate for breakfast, will you sit with me while I eat mine?" he offered a compromise.

"Fine—provided I can have a taste of whatever you order," she teased.

"No way! I'd probably go to work starving if you ever got a fork on my plate!"

Joy enjoyed the free and easy rapport they had established.

"What are you planning to work on today?" Brett asked as he sipped his orange juice.

"I've had an idea for a design ever since my first day in Boca, but I haven't had much luck in getting it down on paper. Maybe today everything will click, and I can finish it."

"Do you enjoy your work, Joy?" he inquired.

"Yes and no. I've always enjoyed designing dresses, but since Mother died, I've had to take over the management of the entire boutique. She used to take me with her on buying trips, but I just went along to see the clothes and accessories. I had no idea how she decided what to buy and how many. She handled all of the business details. I feel so inadequate when it comes to the shoppe's management. It's hard to forget those problems when I try to be creative. My mind is just one, big, gray fog." Joy frowned slightly as she spoke.

"Joy, I'm not a psychologist, but it sounds to me as if you've had so much on your shoulders that you are just depressed—and with good reason. Who wouldn't be after all you have been through? I think you're on the right track with this trip. The sunshine and surroundings are a big change from the cold, rainy weather we were having back home. Just give yourself some time. I wish I could help."

Sympathy for the lovely young woman sitting across from him flooded Brett.

"I appreciate that. Really, I do. But it's something that no one else can do for me. I have to work it out in my own way. You have done a lot by helping me laugh again."

"Happy to be of service, ma'am." Brett exaggerated his own slight Southern drawl, hoping for a smile. This time it worked as Joy's expression slowly changed from a frown into a small but sunny smile.

"Brett, how can anyone be 'down in the dumps' when they are with you?"

"Ah jus' aim to please, honey chile." Once again he was rewarded with a flash of even, white teeth.

Brett glanced at his Rolex. Reluctantly he said, "I hate to leave, but if I sit here enjoying your company much longer, Sam will think that I'm not coming to work today."

"Is the work on the condo going all right?" Joy queried.

"Yeah, it's a little slow, but we are beginning to iron out some of the problems. By the way, I hope to be back here for dinner tonight. Would you and the McAlisters join me for dinner at the Beach Club?" Brett asked casually.

"I really have wanted to go over there. I'll ask Marianna and let you know when you get in this afternoon." Joy felt a glow of anticipation.

"I'll call you as soon as I get back. Hope you can make it," Brett said as he rose to leave. He winked at her and started for the door.

Joy sat at the table for a few more moments, sipping a fresh cup of coffee and letting her thoughts wander. Last night had boosted her spirits considerably. It had been such a long time since she had experienced that kind of relaxed conversation with friends. Brett had become a part of the group as easily as if he had always known them. But what did he want of her? Was she seeing too much of him? Giving him false hope that she might possibly fall in love with him? Was she even capable of loving anyone at this point in her life? And if she could love again, was it worth the pain that always followed the loss of the loved one?

Joy pondered these disturbing questions as her coffee grew cold. No, she would be better off in the long run if she never opened her heart to anyone again. What she needed was a platonic friendship, whatever that indefinable phrase meant. She would have to fight the warmth that was growing more pronounced each time she was near Brett.

Sitting at the lovely antique desk under the two large windows in her room, Joy looked intently at the Banyan tree. She turned to her art pad and sketched a series of long, crisp lines. The emerald green Oriental dress began to take shape. Her pencil moved swiftly and surely. The touches of scarlet, slashing down the dress and around the mandarin collar, like the flash of the cardinal against the Banyan tree, were dramatic and bold. Joy preferred to execute her drawings in color after the lines of the dress had been firmly established. Now, she thought, if she could just find the exact green silk jacquard fabric she pictured so clearly in her mind . . .

Why hadn't she thought of it before? The inspiration came to Joy with sudden clarity. The dress would be a perfect foil for Elayna DuRant's olive complexion, long jet-black hair, and eyes resembling well-polished jade. Joy brightened noticeably. Elayna had just the coloring and figure to wear this floor-length Oriental creation. She would look even more exquisite than usual—her eyes changing from jade to emerald. Elayna would be so pleased! She loved exotic and startling clothes.

Joy wrote Elayna's name at the top of the drawing. Relief flooded her. With one design completed, she had successfully cleared the first hurdle. It was especially rewarding since Elayna had already placed her order for a dress to wear to the Hospital Ball next year. It was a start—a very small start.

The morning passed so rapidly that it was well past noon before Joy realized she had not called Marianna. She had been so engrossed in her work that all other thoughts had been blocked from her mind. Ah, that was a good sign, too. It had been months since she had been able to free her mind for such intense concentration.

Marianna answered the telephone on the first ring.

"I'm so sorry that I didn't call this morning. I got so caught up in my work that the time slipped by before I knew it," Joy apologized.

"Don't worry about it a minute. I've been sitting in the sun trying to get as much tan as possible before going home. Are you planning to work this afternoon, too?"

"No, I'm through for the day," Joy replied. "Things went better than I had hoped and I want to quit while I'm ahead. By the way, I saw Brett in the dining room this morning. He wanted to know if you and Dan would have dinner with us at the Beach Club tonight."

"That sounds like fun! But are you sure the two of you wouldn't like to have dinner alone? You don't need us old married folks as chaperones," Marianna teased.

"I just met the man! I'm certainly not interested in the

least in a romantic entanglement right now." Joy wondered if her words were entirely true. "Will you come? Please."

"Of course—if you're sure we won't be in the way. What time?"

"About eight, I imagine. But he's going to call me when he gets in, and I'll let you know later."

"That's fine. What do you plan to wear? I haven't been to the Beach Club yet, so I don't know how they dress for dinner."

"I haven't either, but we will probably see everything from long formals to short dresses. You'll look great no matter what you wear."

Marianna chuckled, "Thanks for the vote of confidence, but you are being partial to an old friend, I'm afraid. Call me after you talk with Brett."

"I'll do that," Joy replied.

She stood up, stretched, and walked into the closet to select her ensemble for the evening. After several rejections, she chose a feather-light dress with soft folds of fabric draped to shape a surplice-style bodice that left her shoulders bare. The short, circular skirt would swirl around her legs as she walked or danced. Its soft, lilac color gave the dress an even more delicate and feminine appearance. Carefully she hung it to one side and placed a pair of high-heeled sandals on the floor below the dress. Her lacy lingerie and evening bag were placed on the top of the chest-of-drawers. Having dispensed with those details which would save last-minute frustrations, she slipped into a jonquil yellow swimsuit, added a cover-up, and headed for the pool for a well deserved break.

After a strenuous swim, the delicious warmth of the sun further relaxed her aching muscles. Joy stretched and moved into a more comfortable position on the chaise. It wouldn't do to get a sunburn. She stood and raised the back of the lounge chair so that she could watch the activity going on around her. Only moments after she was settled, a hand holding a yellow flower was thrust in front of her. Startled, she turned to find Brett at her side.

"You looked just like a yellow buttercup sitting there. All you lack is a buttercup for your hair." He grinned like a small boy carrying a bouquet of wildflowers.

"You're crazy, do you know that?" Joy laughed. "That's not a buttercup—it's a yellow hibiscus."

"It doesn't matter what it's called—I just thought it would look great tucked behind your ear." He studied her face thoughtfully. "Now which side signifies that you're spoken for?"

"I don't know. Why do you ask?"

"I just wanted to be sure the guys stayed away." He placed the flower carefully over her right ear and tenderly stroked her hair before moving away.

Ignoring the obvious intent of his comment, Joy grinned in spite of herself. "Thank you! Now maybe all those men who have been hanging around all afternoon will disappear," she said, looking around as if to dismiss the invisible admirers. "Now, tell me, how was *your* day?" she asked.

"Great, really great! It got off to such a good start at breakfast that nothing could have possibly gone wrong. Are you game for a race in the pool?"

"I'm afraid not. I swam twenty laps earlier, and I think that's my limit. You go ahead and I'll watch. But please do me a favor. Don't yell, 'Hey look, Mom!' I've heard that at least a dozen times from every kid who has been in the pool," Joy laughed.

He walked to the diving board, stood poised for a moment, then, with a devilish grin, called to Joy, "Hey, look

Mom! No hands!'' He executed a perfect 'cannonball,' tucking his knees to his chest and entering the pool with a wild splash.

Joy's laugh bubbled from deep within. That felt so good, she thought. When was the last time she had really laughed from the very depths of her being? Brett was better than the tranquilizers the doctor had prescribed immediately after her parents' death. With him around, there would be no need for them at all.

She studied his body as he emerged from the pool and walked back to the diving board. He was very well built. An unusually broad chest and shoulders slanted upward to a muscular neck that must have been developed by a great deal of exercise and probably some weight lifting. His navy blue swimsuit revealed a trim waist and hips. Joy noticed with approval his straight, muscular legs. Funny, hadn't it always been the men who admired women's legs? Nevertheless, those were good-looking legs, she insisted silently.

The water clinging to Brett's body caused every muscle to glisten as if covered with oil. Joy became aware of a strange sensation in her chest as she watched him. It was as if a giant hand had squeezed her heart and stopped it for a moment. When it was released, it hammered at twice its normal speed, as if to recapture the missing beats. She gasped. She could never remember having felt this way before. Brett's undeniable attraction was indefinable. He stirred feelings within her that were both delicious and disturbing.

Her eyes were riveted on him. The sunlight playing on his thick, dark hair turned it to red-gold. Heavy brows emphasized the luminous, brown eyes. Unquestionably Brett McCort was a handsome man by any standards. But Joy knew that, beneath the attractive exterior, was also a compassionate and caring person. She had taken note of his thoughtfulness and the sincere desire to bring happiness. She wondered about his religious background. Perhaps, someday, she would have an opportunity to ask him . . .

Joy mentally gave herself a hearty shake. She was appraising the man as if she were a schoolgirl with her first crush. She scolded herself soundly.

A young child brought her back to reality with his cry, "Hey, Mom, watch me!" Joy laughed with delight and relief. Brett had also heard the small voice and was laughing with her as he flopped in exhaustion on the lounge chair next to hers.

"Did Marianna say that she and Dan could join us tonight?"

"Yes, she had been hoping to go to the Beach Club before they left. But they will need to know the time," Joy replied, having at last curbed her runaway emotions.

The two of them agreed that eight o'clock would be best. In deference to Dan's schedule, they decided not to make the evening a late one.

As the sun began to set, there was a sudden chill in the air. Joy shivered as she stepped into her jump suit and zipped it up to her chin.

"I'd better get going. It will take me quite awhile to get my hair unsnarled and presentable for dinner, unless you want me to go looking like this," She pirouetted and posed before him in an exaggerated model's stance.

"You look fine to me, Buttercup, but I don't think the maitre d' would take kindly to your present state," he grinned.

"In that case, I'll see you later." She tossed the words over her shoulder as she walked rapidly past the Tower and back to the Cloister.

Brett watched her until she had disappeared from sight.

She was really quite a woman, he thought. What was it that had mesmerized him after such a short acquaintance? He had known many beautiful, charming, and intelligent women in his time, but there was something about Joy that he couldn't resist. He had thought about it all day. She had made it very clear that she wasn't ready for a romantic relationship. Yet he seemed to be falling in love with her. He wasn't looking for a brief encounter. He wanted to marry her—to take care of her for the rest of her life.

As the sun set over the Cloister, he watched the clouds turn into brilliant pink cotton balls and the sky explode with a myriad of flaming colors. The vivid colors reminded him of this unusual woman who had entered his life so suddenly and had illuminated his being. *Oh Joy, I wish that I could light up your life as you have mine,* he thought.

Finally he rose, hoping to give his whirling thoughts time to rest before he saw her again. He would have to be very careful not to push her. She might run from him like a frightened little rabbit. No, he must bide his time. Only one thing was certain. He fully intended to marry Joy Lawrence. And he was willing to wait—as long as it took.

CHAPTER 8

JOY, BRETT AND THE McAlisters boarded the shuttle bus at the entrance of the Cloister for the short ride to the Boca Beach Club. Brett pointed out the statue of Pan at the entrance to the courtyard and insisted that Joy tell the story of the legendary musician. By the time her tale had ended, they had crossed the Intracoastal Waterway and were approaching Highway, A1A, paralleling the Atlantic.

Joy commented on the number of condominiums that had been built on the beaches of the Gold Coast since her last visit. "They are lovely, but they do block the view of the ocean," she said with a wry look. "I always enjoyed riding on this highway and looking at the ships far out on the horizon. You could tell if the ocean were rough or calm by the number of whitecaps in the distance."

"Hey, lady, don't knock the condos!" Brett objected. "After all, people need a place to live and architects like me need jobs designing them."

"I know, and I can see both sides of the question, but progress does require sacrifices of one kind or another. I guess you can't have your cake and eat it, too. Maybe I am too much of a sentimentalist, but I wish we could hold onto more of the rich traditions of the past.''

Their debate was interrupted as they neared the entrance to the Beach Club. The gateman waved the shuttle through and soon they were alighting from the bus in front of the restaurant. Marianna and Joy immediately spied the shops that lined the walkway leading to the dining room and walked over to look at the window displays.

Dan turned to Brett and said, ''You haven't been married, so you haven't learned yet that you never ask a woman to dinner where there are stores nearby unless you have plenty of time. Thank heaven, the shops are closed! Otherwise we probably wouldn't get to eat until midnight! By the way, how did the work go today?''

''Not so good. There has been a delay in the delivery of some materials. So, we're going to have to close down for several days. I'll probably be taking the early flight back to Atlanta in the morning to take care of some things in the office while we're waiting,'' Brett explained.

''Marianna and I will be leaving in the afternoon,'' Dan said. ''I have a few more things to finish up at the Gulfstream Bank building in the morning and then we'll head for home. This hasn't been much of a vacation for me, but I'm glad Marianna was able to get away for a few days. With all of the bad weather, she'd been having to stay pretty close to home, and she really needed a change of pace.''

''Did I hear my name mentioned? And what were you saying?'' Marianna asked, as she and Joy returned from their short window-shopping jaunt.

''Honey, how could any comment about you be anything but spectacular?'' Dan teased.

''Better watch it! You'll be back to cold beans and franks

93

before you know it. There is no chef in *our* kitchen like the ones here,'' Marianna said.

Dan put his arm around his pretty wife, and kissed her soundly. ''Mmm, kisses like that will build up brownie points very quickly,'' she told him as she snuggled against him.

Starting toward the dining room, Brett followed Dan's lead. He put his arm around Joy's waist and bent to give her a kiss. Joy surprised him with a bright smile.

The maitre d' led them to a table overlooking the ocean. The view was superb. Even though it was dark outside, the floodlights picked up the whitecaps as they rolled toward the shoreline. There the water quickly lost its frothy topping and flowed rapidly back into the Atlantic, where it was churned once again into a white torrent. The four diners watched in silent awe, pondering the power and beauty of the ocean.

When the captain approached with the oversized menus, he explained how the fish of the day was prepared and gave them additional information about appetizers and entrées. As he left they opened the menus and studied them carefully.

''Do you think they could fix me a good burger and fries?'' Brett asked, without cracking a smile.

''You can't be serious!'' Joy scolded. ''With all of these delicacies on the menu, you want a burger?''

''But, Joy, the menu is printed in French. Remember my 'limited education.' If I ordered, I might get fried grasshopper or something equally nauseating,'' Brett said.

''Don't be silly! Just look at the small print under the French words. It tells you in plain English not only what the item is, but how it is prepared.'' Joy laughed, knowing that he was teasing her again.

Later, Brett listened with pride as Joy placed her order in

what he assumed must be very good French, because the waiter wrote down her selections without question. After the waiter had removed the menus and walked away, he couldn't resist asking, "Did you notice that Joy ordered in French so that I wouldn't know how much she was planning to eat tonight?" The standing joke brought a round of chuckles. Even Joy was amused.

"Do you guys feel a little out-of-place in your conservative business suits?" Marianna changed the subject. I have never seen men wearing such bright outfits in my life. Today, while I was shopping, I saw one man in a yellow jacket and slacks. And his tie looked like a rainbow," she giggled. "But that's not all. There was one wearing a jump suit made from some pink-and-green tropical print. Can you picture that in one of your offices?"

"Hey, no fair! We guys have to break out of our shells occasionally. After all, you girls can wear those bright colors all the time. In these exotic surroundings, even the 'wallflowers' are knockouts!" Dan quipped.

The amiable conversation was interrupted during the meal by appropriate moans and groans as each course was completed and another begun. Joy's plate was watched with interest, to see just what she had ordered. True to her reputation she devoured her appetizer, Nage de Fruit de Mer Florentine, which, she explained, was a combination of oysters, mussels, and clams on spinach, topped with a white wine sauce. This was followed by a salad and cream-of-asparagus soup.

"Don't you think you had better dance off some of those calories before your entrée comes?" Brett asked as he rose, taking for granted that she would welcome a short respite.

"Delighted, sir!" she replied.

Joy smiled at Brett as they walked toward the parquet dance floor. She admired the way he moved—casually, but with dignity. And he did look very dignified tonight, she thought, in a heather brown suit, white-on-white striped shirt, and an amber silk Rooster tie. Then her heart began to hammer, and a knot formed in her throat. In spite of her best intentions, she could not control the attraction she felt for him.

The orchestra that was playing at the Cabana dining room was excellent. Brett took Joy's hand and whirled her into an intricate dance step. Then he held her lightly while they savored the music.

What a delicious feeling it was to be held like this, she reflected. John had been so undemonstrative, using affection only to further his interests. Joy doubted that they would ever have had a compatible and loving relationship. Well, thank goodness, he was out of her life forever. She pitied the poor girl who would take her place in John's life.

She cast a quick glance at Brett. What was it about this man that she found so hard to resist in spite of her determination not to yield to her emotions. Brett took her hand and placed it on his other shoulder. With his right arm still holding her tightly, he outlined the contours of Joy's face with his free hand. The touch of his fingers on her face sent lightning bolts of excitement down her spine.

She closed her eyes and listened in silence as the band began to play "their song." Her life had been undeniably brightened by this man who was a stranger until only a few, short days ago. She wished that time could stand still and she could hold onto the delicious feelings that enveloped her.

The fragrance of Brett's cologne wafted about her in a most sensual way. She knew that it was sandalwood, but there was something different—perhaps a blend of the essence itself and the unique chemical reaction of Brett's body. The aroma clung to her, awakening dormant sensations she had refused to acknowledge until now.

Time had passed so quickly that the orchestra had stopped for a break before Joy was aware that there was no longer any music. She pulled away from Brett and looked into his eyes. Their shimmering amber flecks were more prominent than ever, and she sensed that he could see into the very depths of her soul—that he could read her thoughts. She must guard her private world very carefully.

"Let's pretend the music hasn't stopped and stay here until the orchestra comes back," Brett whispered.

"I don't think that would be too smart. People would probably think that we were the floor show and start to throw tomatoes at us if we just stood here looking at each other," she said with a grin.

"I suppose you're right . . ." He still held her tightly. "Then how about a walk on the beach after we eat? We can send the chaperones back to the Cloister."

"You are the most determined man I ever met! Have you always gotten everything you wanted?" Joy asked.

"Everything that was worth having," Brett confessed. "I had to work hard for all of the good things, but they are important enough to me that I didn't mind the hard work. Now, don't change the subject. Will you go for a walk with me?"

"Your powers of persuasion are too much for me. I give up," Joy said.

"Hey, I like the sound of that!" Brett said brightly, but his smile faded as he saw her reproachful look.

"Don't get me wrong," he continued quickly. "I only meant that I'm glad you agreed to the walk. No ulterior motives intended, I assure you."

Hand-in-hand, they strolled toward their table, admiring the triple-tiered atrium design of the room. The waning moon could be seen through the skylights and banks of windows that were built into the ultra-modern building.

Verdant runners from hundreds of philodendron plants cascaded like waterfalls from one of the levels that soared above them. Palms and tropical greenery were placed at strategic points throughout the room to break the stark white expanse of the room. Joy loved the plants and the view afforded by the extensive use of glass. Brett, particularly, was appreciative of the unusual architectural design.

"Isn't it strange that everyone in this room would probably describe this place differently?" Joy mused.

"The old saying that beauty is in the eye of the beholder applies to things as well as to people, Joy. Now, I like the appearance of this structure, but I know you really don't care for modern architecture. You probably think of it as just another obstacle to the beauty of nature, just like you feel about the condos on the beach." Brett summarized their differing views.

"Let's not start on that again. No one has been able to solve that problem yet, and I don't think that we will be able to solve it tonight." Joy ended any further conversation which might spoil the warmth she felt toward this man who was becoming so important to her.

The remainder of the meal was accompanied by cheerful conversation and more chuckles as Joy devoured her poached filet of snapper with lobster sauce and vegetables. When the waiter came to take their dessert orders and displayed the luscious desserts from which they could make their selections, Brett turned to Joy.

"And what kind of sherbet will you have?" he asked.

Joy wrinkled her brow in deep thought. Finally she said, "I believe I'll try the raspberry mousse."

The faces of Joy's companions registered utter disbelief! Even with all of the good-natured teasing about her appetite, they could not fathom her ability to eat dessert after such a meal. She proved them wrong shortly when she finished the last bite and then accepted chocolate after-dinner mints. They were all still laughing when they emerged from the restaurant.

"By the time she goes home, she will have gained twenty pounds," Brett grinned.

"Well, frankly, I'm glad to see her eating so well. She looked too thin when I first saw her," Marianna added her opinion.

"Don't worry. When I gain five pounds, I'll cut back," Joy assured them. "After all, I'm the one who has to do the cooking at home. So, I plan to take advantage of the cuisine while I'm here."

Brett turned to the McAlisters and said, "Joy had promised to take a walk on the beach with me. We'll work off a few calories so that she can eat everything she wants tomorrow."

"You two go for your walk. Frankly, I'm bushed and we have to get up early to pack for the trip home tomorrow," Dan said.

"Oh, no! Are you and Marianna really leaving so soon?" Joy moaned in disappointment.

"Yes, I'm afraid so. I just have one or two loose ends to tie up in the morning. Then it's back to the old grind," Dan told her.

Joy hugged him and then turned to Marianna. "You have been a lifesaver to me. I'm so glad that we had this time to renew our friendship."

"It's been wonderful, Joy. Do call when you get home, and we'll go out for lunch," Marianna smiled, unable to resist one last mention of food.

With affectionate embraces all around, the McAlisters boarded the shuttle bus for the ride back to the Cloister. Joy's eyes welled with tears, and her chin began to quiver slightly as she watched her friends drive away. She had just rediscovered an old friend at a time when she needed her most. Now she was leaving and Joy felt a sense of loss.

Brett put a comforting arm around her and studied her face carefully. He thought she looked like a porcelain doll with crystal tears rolling down her face. Sensing that her emotions were very fragile, he tried valiantly to control his own.

Slowly he pulled Joy to him and kissed her tenderly. The gentle kiss began to ease some of her pain, and she found herself responding with a fervor that surprised them both. She clasped her arms about him as if he were a life preserver tossed to a victim of shipwreck. Her eager response kindled his desire. He kissed her deeply and she answered with warmth and longing.

Reluctantly they parted and strolled toward the beach.

CHAPTER 9

JOY QUICKLY FOUND that walking on the beach while wearing high-heeled sandals was not only very difficult but a little ridiculous. Brett supported her as she removed first one and then the other. Taking the sandals, he poked one in each of his coat pockets, then removed his coat and slung it carelessly over his shoulder. With his arm around her slim waist, they began to walk down the beach. Joy's head rested against his strong shoulder.

They ambled along in silence for a short distance, unaware that they were headed in the direction of the Boca Raton Inlet. They soon discovered that their progress had been halted by the span of water which poured into the ocean.

"If we want to go any further south, we'll have to swim across the mouth of the inlet," Joy laughed at her astonished escort.

"I had forgotten that it was so close to the Beach Club. The hotel is surrounded on three sides by water." Brett was chagrined.

Hoping to temper his disappointment, Joy spoke. "They say that this is where Boca Raton got its name. Apparently some seventeenth-century Spanish sailors thought that the mouth of the channel with its sharp pointed rocks resembled the teeth in a rat's mouth. *Boca Raton* means 'mouth of the rat' in English." Joy grinned as he wrinkled his nose in distaste.

"That has to be the most unromantic thing any woman has ever said to a man while strolling along the beach on a beautiful, moonlight night. But I like the Spanish pronunciation the 'locals' use—making 'Raton' rhyme with 'stone.'"

"There are some interesting stories about the harbor, too," Joy continued. "It is said that pirates once hid their ships inside the rocks so that they could dash out and capture vessels carrying gold and treasure, and even beautiful women. I can just picture you as a pirate with a cutlass in your teeth, jumping from one ship to another. You would probably have grabbed the fairest of the damsels and carried her back to your ship. She would have fallen madly in love with you and followed you gladly back to Spain or Portugal!" Joy's imagination ran rampant with images of earlier days.

"Aha, I like the picture you are conjuring up! So, I'm a pirate grabbing a beautiful lady and bodily carrying her away with him, huh? Perhaps . . . like this?" He swept Joy up in his arms and ran with her a few yards up the beach.

"No, Brett! Put me down! That was just make-believe. Put me down!"

"But I want to make all of your fantasies come true, Princess. So I'm going to carry you off to a deserted island and we will live there happily forever and ever." He laughed as she vigorously but vainly tried to escape.

Abandoning her efforts, she was unable to keep from

joining in his laughter. Exhausted from their spirited tussle, Joy began to relax in his arms. He held her easily. She felt no heavier than a child, he thought. As their laughter subsided, Brett bent his head slowly to hers and moved his lips softly over her forehead to her ear. His deep breathing ruffled her hair as it spilled around her shoulders. She wrapped her soft arms around his neck as his lips tenderly sought hers.

Brett showered Joy's face with kisses, his lips lingering at the hollow of her throat where the pulse pounded erratically. Through the soft fabric of his shirt, Joy could feel his heart beating in tempo with her own. He kissed her once again and she sensed his growing desire. Powerless against the fever his kisses ignited in her, she reveled in the exquisite agony.

Uttering a low moan Brett released her decisively, setting her down. As Joy's feet touched the sandy beach, she became conscious that her knees would no longer support her body. Brett held her gently as she spread her shawl and settled on the beach. Then he dropped down to sit beside her. With the moonlight bathing their faces in its soft glow, they watched the relentless pounding of the surf, reflecting their own rising passions.

At last Brett spoke, his voice husky. "Joy, I almost lost control a minute ago, and I love you too much for a casual affair. You're too important to me."

Joy breathed deeply, exhaling in a long sigh of relief. "Thank you, Brett, for caring that much." Her gratitude was intensified by the knowledge that it was he who had regained his composure long enough to halt the rushing tide of emotions that had threatened to sweep them both away.

"Believe me, that was one of the hardest things I've ever had to do. I want you so much, but not like this," he answered. Then seeking an avenue that would relieve some of his pain, he continued, "But don't involve me in any more of your fantasies. I began to pretend that I was the pirate kidnapping you and, suddenly, I was living the part. If I had had a ship, you would have been halfway to the Bahamas by now!"

She laughed in relief, as a sense of normality returned. Joy straightened the soft swirls of her dress and retrieved her shawl which now resembled a beach blanket instead of a couturier's dream.

Brushing the last grains of sand from her dress, Joy opened her evening bag and found a comb to run through her hair. Then she made an attempt to repair her make-up.

"You look great without any of that," Brett smiled fondly as she touched her lips with gloss.

He shook her large shawl vigorously, letting the ocean breeze carry away the last vestige of sand. Then he lovingly wrapped it around her shoulders and pulled her to him for one last embrace before they left the shore. Holding her closely to him, they walked toward the entrance where they would catch the shuttle to the Cloister.

As they rode past the fountain on their return, Brett turned to Joy. "Let's don't end the evening just yet. How about a walk in the courtyard?"

Sharing his reluctance to break the spell of this perfect evening, Joy quickly agreed. They walked slowly, admiring the citrus trees with their tiny, twinkling lights. The colored spotlights focusing on the fountain bathed "The Lady" in a myriad of changing hues, adding dimension and depth to the crystal water spilling forth. The statue stood, proud and serene above them, her secret safe behind her enigmatic smile.

"I love this place," Joy said. "The Garden of Eden itself could not have been more exquisitely beautiful."

"Perhaps this *is* the Garden of Eden. At least you are my

Eve—my lovely little temptress. There are times when you frustrate me, puzzle me, tease me, delight me—but you are worth the risk.''

Brett had seated himself beside Joy on one of the glazed tile benches that were positioned to offer the best view of the fountain. Now he looked into her face. She could feel his eyes, like little fingers of heat, caressing her. She turned toward the source of the warmth, her heart in her throat.

''Joy, you must know how much I love you.'' He stared intently into her sparkling, aquamarine eyes and pondered how to tell her that he must go to Atlanta the following day. He would miss her as if she were a limb that had been severed from his body. She had become a part of his very being during the few short days he had known her.

Joy found it impossible to speak. Her emotions were at such a peak that she was afraid to chance a reply. Her body began to tingle once more with the memory of Brett's embrace. What had happened to her? She had known this man only a few days; yet, tonight, she had tossed her inhibitions to the wind and succumbed to his passionate kisses. What could she have been thinking to let such a thing happen? She had been so determined that she would not become involved with anyone again. Yet she sat quivering under his steady gaze—his velvety, brown eyes almost hypnotic in their effect on her.

Sheer physical attraction had caused her to react the way she had on the beach—a release from long pent-up emotions, she decided. It must not happen again, or she would be trapped by her own emotions. What had Brett said about ''risk''? He was ready to risk—to be vulnerable. She was not. And she must not give her newly discovered passion any further opportunity for expression.

''Joy, did you hear me?'' Brett was saying. ''I said that I love you! You are the one I have waited for all these years. I realize we haven't known each other long, but I want to marry you. I want you to be my wife.''

The color drained from Joy's face, nerves tensed as if she had received a sudden blow to her body. Surely she had misunderstood Brett. He couldn't have asked her to marry him. Why would he do that just as she was beginning to get her head together and they were building a comfortable relationship? She felt herself spinning dizzily, pulled against her will into a violent whirlpool of doubts and fears.

''Brett, you know I can't marry you.'' Her reply sounded harsh even to her own ears, though she had not intended it so. ''You knew that I needed some time to adjust, to work some things out for myself. ''Please—don't rush me!''

Brett's dark eyes clouded. He rose abruptly, towering over her. His face was contorted with pain and anger.

''I don't believe you, Joy! You felt the same way I did down on the beach. Don't bother to deny it! I don't want to have a casual affair with you. I want to marry you—yet you treat my proposal like an insult. I can't stand much more of this torture—of being with you and not having you. Tonight I thought you were finally ready to climb out of your dark cave and join the rest of the human race. But I was wrong—very wrong. Well, don't worry! I won't be around to intrude on your privacy. You can be alone to your heart's content. Please excuse me if I don't escort you to your room. Since you are so intent on doing things on your own, you can find your way, I'm sure. Good night!''

Brett's words, like physical blows, forced the breath from her body, leaving her speechless and battered.

He turned on his heel and stalked angrily toward the hotel, not waiting to hear Joy's explanation—that she didn't want to risk hurting him or being hurt until she had sorted out her other problems. And now she faced the most stag-

106

gering realization of all—that she did, indeed, love Brett McCort! Joy could see nothing but lights swimming in a pool of water as tears flowed in dark rivulets down her face. Her breathing became labored and she sobbed uncontrollably.

Curling up on the bench, she cried until she was exhausted. Her sobs became dry rasping gasps. When all of her tears were spent, she could not will her body to stand. Staring at the fountain, she raised her swollen eyes to the "Lady of Boca." What was her secret? How could she smile when Joy's world was crumbling around her?

Finally Joy rubbed her eyes so that she could look at her watch. She discovered that she had been lying on the hard tile for over two hours. Her body ached all over, but the pain she felt within her made the other seem insignificant. With the corner of her shawl, she wiped her mascara-stained face. Quietly she slipped into the lobby and up to her room, hoping no one would notice her disheveled appearance.

Walking into the bathroom, she stripped off the lovely dress that was now soiled with both sand and make-up, and dropped it in the middle of the floor. Her delicate, lace-trimmed underclothes followed. When she had undressed, she walked across the clothing as if it were not there, and stepped into the shower. Icy spears of water stung her face and body. She had hoped that they would wake her sleeping brain so that she could make some sense of the evening. The water washed away the dark streaks from her face, but she made no attempt to move.

Questions ran through Joy's mind. Why had she been left when everyone she had ever loved had been taken? Why did she have to endure life without them? Was this the reason she had refused to let herself love again, why it was so difficult to say the words *I love you?* Was this a punishment for something she had done? Why did God seem so very far away—now, of all times, when she needed Him most.

The icy water finally took its toll on Joy's body, and she began to shake violently. Turning the water off, she reached for a towel, dripping water on the pile of clothes as she walked across it once more. Toweling herself dry, she grabbed the first gown she could find, slid it over her head, and fell across the bed.

Raising her head for a moment she listened intently, hoping to hear some sound from Brett's room. There was only deathly silence, though the sound of his angry accusations reverberated through her brain. Ironically, "their" song played inharmoniously in the background, spinning around and around like a broken record. The words and melody were haunting. The light had left her life, but the music lingered on.

Suddenly Joy's eyes fell on Ellen's Bible. She had placed it on the bedside table when unpacking on that first day. It had not been opened since. Now she found herself fingering the pages, velvety from much use, scanning once-familiar passages:

The Lord is my shepherd, I shall lack for nothing.
He makes me lie down in green pastures, he leads me
*   beside quiet waters, he restores my soul . . .*

Could it have been the Lord who had brought her to this place of green tranquillity and still waters—to be restored, renewed? The Psalmist continued:

I will be glad and rejoice in your love, for you saw my
*   affliction and know the anguish of my soul . . .*

Her Creator knew her so well. He had seen her tears, her aching heart, her anguished soul—and He loved her in spite of her fragile faith!

I sought the Lord, and he answered me, he delivered me
  from all my fears.

Had she really sought the Lord? Or was she, as Brett had insisted, still intent on working things out for herself? Well, she had to admit, she had certainly made a royal mess of things. She read on:

Delight yourself in the Lord and he will give you the
  desires of your heart.

Was this marvelous promise really hers? The desires of her heart—a love-filled marriage, children—seemed more remote than ever. When Brett walked out, her heart had almost stopped beating. Yet the promise was preceded by a condition—"Delight yourself in the Lord." That was it! Her priorities were badly out of order. Here in Boca she had been seeking rest for her body and mind when what she really needed was rest for her spirit. She buried her face in the pages of Ellen's Bible and wept. This time, the tears were tears of repentance and healing.

Feeling somewhat refreshed, Joy stepped into the bathroom to wash her tear-stained face. Her innately tidy nature recoiled at the sight of the sodden pile of clothing still lying on the bathroom floor. She bent down and scooped up the armload of silky fabric, and then she smelled the fragrance —sandalwood. The scent clung to the dress she had worn, assailing her senses, invading her heart and mind.

She must see Brett again—if only to apologize for her strange behavior. Somehow, whatever the future held for them, Joy knew she would never be completely alone again.

CHAPTER 10

THE SUN WAS ALREADY shining brightly when Joy opened her swollen eyelids. She was groggy from the after-effects of the traumatic evening, but her heart was lighter. Today she would make things right with Brett. She must dress quickly and talk with him before he left for work.

Taking almost no thought of her appearance, she grabbed the pink jump suit and stepped into it hurriedly. Rather than flattering her complexion, the bright color emphasized its pallor. There was nothing that she could do to remove the puffiness from her face, but at least she could try to hide the chalky whiteness, broken by the large indigo circles under her eyes. She slathered on foundation, more blush than usual, and touched a bright pink lipstick to her lips. All of her efforts were insufficient to cover the devastation of the evening before. Only her eyes revealed a new serenity.

Dumping the contents from her evening bag into her shoulder tote, she then picked up the key which she had slung across the desk the night before and rushed toward the elevator. Surely, she thought, she would be able to catch

Brett before he left the dining room. Everything would be all right if she could just speak with him.

As she walked into the lobby, she glanced out the tall, arched windows and saw Brett. He was wearing a business suit rather than the familiar work garb, and was standing by the airport limo. What was he doing? Where was he going? Why hadn't he told her that he was leaving?

The driver of the limousine had finished stowing the luggage and Brett was climbing into the automobile before she could reach the doors of the hotel. Having run all the way across the long lobby, Joy was breathing heavily as she pushed open the front doors without waiting for the doorman's assistance. Just as she stepped outside, the car pulled away. She wanted to call out to the driver to stop, but the words caught in her throat. It was too late. She stood frozen. But thoughts and questions toppled over each other in an effort to bring some semblance of order to the devastating turn of events.

Brett hadn't told her he was leaving, she was sure of that. Was he so angry with her that he would ignore his job here and just take off without a word of explanation? Where was he going? And why? Why? The questions pounded in her mind like an angry surf, eroding the measure of peace that had come to her through Ellen's Bible.

Once more the tears welled up in her eyes. How could there be any tears left? She turned, walked stiffly back into the hotel, and took the elevator to her floor.

When she reached her room, she fell across the bed. Then she smelled it again . . . the sandalwood cologne. His fragrance lingered, but now he was gone—and this time she had lost him forever!

If she had only controlled her long-denied passions . . . If she hadn't responded to his ardent kisses . . . If he hadn't asked her to marry him—then she would have had more

111

time to straighten out her life—a life that would now never include Brett McCort.

The room became a prison. She prowled about like a caged tiger. The sight of the Banyan tree did nothing to ease her pain, nor did the Bible that lay open to the book of Psalms. Overnight everything had changed. All of the bright beauty had turned to ugly shades of gray and black. She flung herself across the bed and wept tears that had been hidden in some recess of her body only to spring forth anew when it appeared that the supply had been exhausted.

It was almost evening before Joy became aware that she had not eaten in almost twenty-four hours. She called room service and ordered a salad and hot tea. She winced when she thought of the happy dinners she had shared with Brett, and his playful teasing. Well, she had no appetite tonight.

Joy didn't taste a bite of the lovely salad. Robot-like, she lifted the fork to her mouth, chewed, and swallowed. After the waiter had removed the table, she was once more alone with her thoughts. They were anything but good company.

Brett, I love you, she thought. *Please listen to me— wherever you are. I love you. Why can't I speak those words when I'm with you? I'm sure God sent you to me to help me work out my problems just by your presence and understanding. He knew you could teach me to love again. You were a part of the plan all along! Brett, can you hear me? I love you, I love you, I love you . . .*

Golfers dotted the fairways and greens beyond Joy's window, and the groundskeepers were busy with their assigned tasks before she made any attempt to stir. She looked toward the window, and the brilliance of the sun's rays saddened her. How could the sun shine so brightly when her mood was dark and somber? She pulled the sheet over her head and lay motionless. If she did not move, maybe she could erase the memory of the events that had led to this state of black depression. But the more she tried to forget, the more the memories rushed back to haunt her.

With a determined effort Joy pushed back the covers and raised her body to a sitting position. Her legs moved sluggishly and mechanically. Like a zombie she walked toward the bathroom and splashed water on her face. There seemed to be no reason to dress. She located a robe that she had thrown on the floor and struggled to slip it on. Standing in the center of the room, she looked around as if she could not decide where she was and had no idea what she should do next.

The ringing of the phone broke the silence. Its insistent, piercing noise caused Joy's body to jerk involuntarily. She put her hands to her ears in an attempt to stop the deafening sound. Then, hoping it might be Brett, she lifted the receiver.

"Joy, it's Ellen. How are you dear?"

Usually Ellen's voice was mellow and calm, but today there was a distinct note of hysteria.

"Ellen, are you all right? Is Granny Okay?" What's wrong?" Joy was suddenly concerned.

"I'm fine and Granny is fine. But I really do need to talk with you. I was going to call last night, but decided that morning would be a better time," Ellen continued.

"A better time for what?"

"Well, the news is good, but the timing couldn't be worse. All the customers, who were so understanding while we finished the gowns for the hospital balls, are impatient to know when this dress and that dress will be ready. And the mothers of the debutantes are anxious to pick up their

113

daughters' gowns so they can have their portraits done. To top it all off, we are already getting orders for next year's charity balls. They just won't listen to anything I tell them. They want to talk with you—and nobody else. I hated to call you, but my nerves are just about shredded, Joy. When can you come home?'' Ellen's litany of complaints was like salt in an open wound.

"Oh, Ellen, things are not going well for me, either. I haven't had time to relax and I don't feel at all like working.'' Joy's normally gentle voice was high and shrill.

Her friend, concerned with her own problems and the pressures of work, made no comment. Of all people, Joy had expected Ellen to sympathize, but she had seemingly ignored Joy's unspoken plea.

When the older woman continued, Joy grasped her head and pressed her fingers to her throbbing temple: "Ellen . . . Ellen, stop a minute and listen to me. . . . Yes, I know how troublesome they can be. . . . Yes, I'll come home. I'll be on the first flight I can get. This is the peak of the tourist season, you know. . . . No, don't bother to meet me. Just try to hold yourself together for a few more days. If things get too bad, just close the shoppe until I get home. Now, hang up and go fix yourself a cup of hot tea. I'll see you soon.''

Joy replaced the receiver and put her head down on the pillow. What else could go wrong? How much more could she take?

Then her tumbled thoughts focused on an idea that had evolved slowly—ever since the day of the shopping spree with Marianna. In the children's clothing stores, Joy had fingered the dainty batiste day gowns and admired the exquisite smocking on the toddler dresses, and the idea had taken shape. A children's boutique! She was committed to designing the ball gowns for the upcoming social season, but she had always longed to create fashions in miniature

114

—those treasured keepsakes of love that could be handed down from one generation to another. *Such designs only grow more precious and beautiful with time,* she thought, *like fine old silver.*

Joy shook her head impatiently. There would be time later to discuss the idea with Ellen. Right now there was a crisis that demanded every erg of her failing energy. She breathed a prayer for strength, and picked up the phone to make her reservation on the next plane to Atlanta. Just as she had expected, all flights were booked for the next four days. She declined stand-by. If there was anything she disliked, it was being tied to a phone waiting for a ticket agent to report a cancellation.

Her thoughts returned to the conversation with Ellen. Strange that her wise and mature friend should need a shoulder to lean on. Joy had thought her a paragon of strength and faith. *How human we all are,* she mused. Even her beloved parents had not had all the answers, but they had pointed her to the unfailing Source. From that Fountain flowed every resource she would ever need. The realization, however, did not quite remove the pain she still felt at the thought of Brett . . .

Joy did not leave the room for the rest of the day, nor did she bother to eat until late evening when she ordered a light meal of soup and hot tea. The food did little to raise her spirits, but it did slightly dull the throbbing in her head.

She picked up several current magazines she had brought to read and thumbed through the pages. The titles were cruelly ironic: "How to Find Someone Who Will Love You as You Are"; "How to Let Go and Love Again"; "Eight Ways to Tell Whether You Are a Loser in Love"; "How Do You Overcome Your Addiction to Him?"; "Do You Have Enough Initiative to Be Your Own Boss?" When she spotted an article entitled "Living Alone and Having a Ball," Joy flung the magazines into the waste paper basket. No help here. She reached, instead, for Ellen's Bible and turned to the Psalms. David, too, suffered under a heavy burden of his own making.

Later, the quiet of the moonlit night was broken by a bird outside her window, improvising a song of exquisite trills and swells. He poured out the melodious notes, liquid and sweet, in a serenade of ecstasy. Joy had awakened when he began his melodious melody to his mate. It was almost too much to bear, but she listened in reverence to this primitive ritual of love. A phrase from an old song came to her: "His eye is on the sparrow, and I know He watches me." Comforted, she slept.

The next morning Joy showered and dressed, determined to spend a more normal day. Her reflection in the full-length mirror told her she still had a long way to go to recover her customary sparkle.

On her way to the dining room, Domenick inquired if she were feeling ill and asked if there were anything he might do to help. She attempted a weak smile but assured him she would be just fine. His eyes reflected her pain as he watched her slow progress through the lobby.

She picked at her breakfast, eating only a few bites, and then wandered back into the lobby. To pass the time, she decided to browse in DeLoy's, an exclusive boutique offering designer originals, available in this specialty shop alone. Seeing the results of others' creativity might stimulate her own.

Joy admired the fabrics, the workmanship, and the unusual detailing. There was a wide selection of clothing for every type of woman and for any event she might wish to attend.

116

Joy's attention was suddenly drawn to the colors in a skirt of the softest, sheerest georgette she had ever seen. The fabric was designed with vertical stripes of rainbow colors that looked like a watercolor painting. She was impressed by the ingenious way in which the material had been doubled, with the fold at the hemline. By doubling the georgette, the filmy material was not marred by the thickness of a hem. It was so beautiful that Joy replaced it on the rack with a touch of envy. Oh, how she wished to be creative again. She left the lovely little shop and walked out into the lobby.

She considered writing to Brett. Perhaps a letter explaining her attitude would be more effective. She sat down at one of the little desks that were placed at intervals under the tall windows. At any other time, Joy would have reveled in the lovely tropical palms and plants outside the windows, creating a garden paradise. But at the moment Joy was oblivious to everything except the need to communicate with Brett. With the pen poised over the paper, she stared at the blank pink page bearing the golden crest of the hotel. Her mind went blank. She could think of nothing to write! She rose from the desk and trudged back to her room to spend another restless night.

For the first time since Brett's departure, Joy made a valiant attempt to look like her attractive self. She dressed carefully and applied make-up. The mascara made her eyes look wide and haunted. No matter, she thought. There was no longer anyone whom she was trying to please.

She had ignored the aching protest of her stomach when she neglected to eat breakfast. Now it was rumbling noisily. The feasts of previous days now made the famine of the last two days unbearable. Joy walked into the Expresso, hoping that a light lunch would calm the queasiness within.

Ordinarily she would have been entranced by the Victorian dining room with its "gingerbread trim," bentwood chairs, brass railings, and stained-glass panels that glowed colorfully throughout the room. Today, even the most glorious sights could not distract her.

She ordered a bowl of minestrone. Other diners appeared to be enjoying the food, but Joy could not taste a thing. The soup did nothing to warm the cold interior of her body.

When she left the dining room, she strolled aimlessly, finding herself in the courtyard. She had purposely avoided the fountain since her traumatic scene with Brett the night he had walked out of her life. But she needed to see it again. She could not allow this unhappy episode to tarnish the wonderful attachment she had always felt for the Cloister and its surroundings.

Sitting on one of the benches that was shaded by an orange tree, she tried to look at the fountain. Her eyes welled with tears once more and she had to look away. The golden fruit hanging over her head caught her eye. Without thinking, she reached up and plucked one of the oranges. The instant that she did so, she was sorry. She should have left it there for others to enjoy. If every guest picked one piece of fruit, the trees would soon be bare. Well, she thought, since she couldn't put it back, she would eat it.

Her fingernail would not pierce its shiny surface. Turning the orange around in her hand, she studied it intently. So engrossed was she that she did not see the airport limo arrive, nor did she see Brett emerging from the automobile. He, too, had glanced at the statue and the fountain when the car drove past, and had spotted Joy sitting on the bench. He asked the doorman to take care of his luggage and started for the fountain when he noticed an elderly gentleman approaching Joy.

Joy, too, had been so caught up in her own thoughts that

she was unaware of the man's presence until he appeared before her. He was a miniature Santa Claus. His lively, blue eyes twinkled, and his full head of snow-white hair and beard were to be envied by Santa himself.

"Young lady," he asked, "would you like to borrow my pocket knife to peel that orange?"

Startled by the voice, Joy looked up into the beaming, friendly face, "Oh, thank you. I would appreciate it."

As the man reached in his pocket, he said, "There is an old superstition about peeling fruit. If you cut off the entire peel without breaking it, turn the peel around three times over your head, and throw it over your shoulder, the paring will form the initial of your lover's name."

He watched as Joy peeled the fruit in one curling ribbon of orange. The jovial, little man wiped the blade of his knife, replaced it in his pocket, and smiled as he strolled away leaving Joy staring at the peel in her hand.

Feeling a little foolish, she circled the peeling around her head three times. *This is silly,* she thought, *a little like kissing the turned-up hem of your skirt in the hope of getting a new dress.* Nevertheless, she tossed it over her shoulder and turned to see a perfectly formed, golden "B" on the ground. She gasped and rushed blindly from the courtyard toward the Banyan tree.

Brett had stood in the shadow of the trees, listening to the conversation. He walked to where Joy had been sitting and looked down to see the initial glowing against the dark earth. He followed the path that Joy had taken, and when he reached the corner of the building, turned and looked for her. It appeared that she had vanished. Then he saw her sitting on the grass with her hands and face pressed against the trunk of the Banyan tree. As he moved closer, he could hear the desperate sobs coming from the small, forlorn figure.

"Joy, honey, don't cry like that. Please don't cry. I can't stand to see you so unhappy," he pleaded.

Jumping up suddenly, she stared at him incredulously. He had come back! He must still care for her! As quickly as the tears had begun, they disappeared, leaving only dark rivers of mascara trailing down her face. A radiant smile transformed her face for the first time in days.

Brett grasped Joy to him and she flung her arms around his neck. His lips crushed hers, hungry for the sweetness of her kisses after the days of separation. Running her fingers through the thick, dark hair at the back of his neck, she found herself inhaling the familiar sandalwood fragrance. But this time *Brett was here!* His closeness was reassuring and comforting.

They held each other as if their very lives depended on the safe harbor they had found in the other's arms. The entire world around them was forgotten.

"Oh, Brett, I thought you were gone forever—that I would never see you again." Joy was ecstatic. "It was so important that I talk to you, explain to you . . ."

"Hold it! Let me go first," Brett interrupted. "Please forgive me for letting my temper run away with me the other night. I'm afraid that is one of my worst faults. I leap before I look and regret it later. I was the one to blame. I should have waited—given you more time. But when I finally found what I had been looking for all my life, I just couldn't help myself. I was afraid that you might slip away from me."

"But I should not have been so abrupt," Joy insisted. "It was just an involuntary reflex—like jerking your hand away from a hot stove. I had been burned so badly once before. I need you, Brett. But it took the shock of your leaving me to make me realize it."

"Honey, I didn't leave you. I had been trying to tell you

all evening that I had business in Atlanta the next day. But I was dreading the separation. As angry as I was at that moment, I never had any intention of leaving you. You will just have to put up with my hanging around until you are ready for me to ask you again to be my wife,'' Brett said as he kissed her cheek gently.

"Oh, Brett, I missed you so much. You don't know what these days without you have been like. I have relived every moment we have spent together. You were right the first day we met when you said that maybe you could help. You see, I think God sent you to me. That may sound strange to you . . . but so many things have happened since I have been here that it *couldn't* be coincidence. I need your strength, your happy disposition, your love. I need *you*.''

He looked longingly into the blue eyes that were now streaked with red, and puffy from hours of crying.

"Joy, please forgive me for hurting you so. When I left, I thought it would be best not to call you—that you needed time alone. It never occurred to me that you would think I had deserted you. I'll try to be patient until you are ready. What you have told me does not surprise me at all. While we were apart, I did my share of praying, too, and I am convinced that God intended us for each other—to love and to cherish.''

He took Joy in his arms once again and kissed her tenderly. As he held her, Joy looked up at the canopy of greenery formed by the branches of the Banyan tree. Then the thought struck her: The characteristics of the Banyan tree—compassion, strength, support, sturdiness, protection, and faith—were all qualities that Brett possessed! He had been the one she had searched for since she was a little girl. With Brett's help she could learn to face the future unafraid.

CHAPTER 11

JOY TOOK GREAT PAINS in selecting the dress she would wear for dinner that evening. After much consideration she decided on an eye-catching, one-shoulder design. She loved to combine unorthodox colors, and the geranium-pink georgette dress with its American Beauty red sash was one of her finest creations. Tonight, above all nights, she wanted to look her very best for Brett.

She had stayed in the sun a little longer than usual after her swim, hoping to turn the pallor of her complexion to a rosy hue. Her smooth skin now glowed.

As Joy deftly applied her make-up, she remembered the one time she had treated herself to a salon evaluation during one of her visits to New York. Her face had been labeled "a fantasy face"—no hard edges—a face of natural beauty, contrived and complicated, but showing strength." The world-famous cosmetician had said, "You love the enchanting . . . the organdies, chiffons, slipper satins, taffeta, draped and flowing in a mist of impressionists' pallets."

Great care had been taken in pressing the dress so that the

folds of the skirt flowed softly from her waist. The luscious pink fabric that draped across her breasts was held by tiny spaghetti ties at one shoulder, and the softness of the lines was enhanced by the startling scarlet sash. The dramatic touch of color added just the right amount of spice to the delicious creation, she thought, as she twirled in front of the mirror. She smiled at the reflection as her skirt rippled in waves about her feet.

Remembering how the fragrance of Brett's cologne had lingered long after he was gone, Joy daubed some perfume behind each ear and at the pulse points of her wrists. Heavy perfumes had never suited her and she had taken great care in selecting this one—a light souffle that was supposed to haunt the wearer and incite curiosity. She hoped that the "Gloria Vanderbilt" perfume would have just that effect on Brett.

She was ready long before she heard Brett's knock. When she opened the door, he stood for a long moment gazing at her in silent admiration.

"Brett!" she breathed his name. He was stunning in a white dinner jacket.

"Hello, Princess." His voice was low and husky as he pulled her toward him. "You are even more beautiful than I remembered."

His slow, sensual kiss sent Joy's pulse racing. She stirred uneasily in his arms, and he moved away, sensing her discomfort.

"Don't be afraid, Joy. You can trust me . . ." Then, in a less serious tone, he said, "I think we had better get you something to eat. You have lost several pounds while I was away. Haven't you been eating?" Brett scolded.

"Well, I guess I lost my appetite . . ."

"In that case, let's go find it. Maybe they will kill the fatted calf for their prodigal guest," he grinned, taking her arm and ushering her ceremoniously from the room.

When they arrived in the Patio Royale, they found it transformed into a coral fantasia by the mellow glow of candlelight. Ornamental fig trees growing in large urns sparkled with tiny, white lights. And Addison Mizner's passion for arches was in evidence throughout the room. Pointed arches framed the soaring windows and tall, white, rounded ones crowned the massive wooden doors. Baskets of ferns were suspended from the center of another row of graceful arches, supported by twin columns that spanned the width of the room.

Joy and Brett were seated on a raised balcony overlooking the main part of the dining room. From the windows they could see a sleek cabin cruiser docking at the hotel's marina on Lake Boca Raton. It was an enchanted evening —a new beginning for them.

Caught up in the spirit of the occasion, Brett said, "Let's celebrate our reunion with a toast." He caught her hand in his and dropped a light kiss in the palm.

"I feel like celebrating! It's so good to have you back. You can't possibly know how lonely it was while you were away," Joy told him.

"You couldn't have been any more unhappy than I. I could just imagine some man sweeping you off your feet before I could get back," he admitted.

"I had to fight them off with a big stick," Joy said as her soft laughter bubbled once again.

She studied the deeply tanned face that had become so precious to her. The cleft in his chin was more prominent by candlelight, and the lines that creased downward beside his mouth deepened with his smile. Then his eyes caught hers. She felt a tingle race up her spine. His eyes affected her in the strangest way. They seemed to caress her face and speak to her in a voice all their own. His eyes had been the first thing she had noticed about him on the drive from the airport. They still intrigued her.

The cooler was placed beside their table and the waiter poured a little of the Perrier in each glass. After the waiter had left the table, Brett raised his glass, "It isn't champagne, but I want to propose a toast to the loveliest lady in the room: Never above you—never below you—always beside you."

As they touched their glasses, Joy looked at him and said, "That was lovely. I don't think I've heard it before."

"It means that I never want to dominate you or be dominated by you, but I'll be there beside you whenever you need me."

"Thank you, Brett," Joy whispered. "Now," she said brightly, "what am I going to have for dinner?"

"Anything you like. Tell me what you want, and I promise I will order for you without comment."

She proceeded to list the items she had selected from the extensive list: Chilled bay shrimp with avocado and grapefruit sections, spinach soup, hearts of lettuce salad with blue cheese dressing, roast Long Island duckling with wild rice and brandied Bing cherries, carrots, and a baked potato.

True to his word, Brett did not utter a word as she named the various foods. But one eyebrow flew up and a sly grin creased his face as he tried to remember her choices. Remarkably he was able to relay the order to the waiter.

Crunching on crispy vegetables from the relish tray before them, they chatted happily. The old happy-go-lucky feeling returned gradually. The tension both of them had felt slowly ebbed away and they lingered over the meal. At times Brett felt himself on the verge of making some comment, but he cautiously refrained. Joy was such a sensitive, beautiful woman and her emotions had been on a seesaw for quite a while. He would have to be very careful not to upset the momentary balance by a careless remark.

Much later, he asked, "Do you want any dessert?"

"If you will have some with me, I'll have some pear sherbet. It's such a delicacy that we can't get it in Atlanta," Joy grinned.

"Only if you'll promise me that afterwards we can go in the El Lago room and hear Van Smith and the band. They're playing there tonight. That guy who plays the trumpet makes me wish I had continued with my trumpet lessons."

"I'd love it!" she agreed.

The elegant room they entered was one that Joy had never seen before, and she swiveled her head to take in all of the decor. The lights in the gleaming chandelier had been dimmed, casting a soft glow over the entire room. She was amazed that such a huge room could feel so cozy. Conversation and laughter mingled with the melodious sound of the orchestra.

The waiter had just pulled out Joy's chair when she felt someone's eyes on her. Turning toward the band, she saw Van Smith at the piano, nodding and smiling. Returning his smile, she settled herself comfortably, and Brett took a seat beside her. Suddenly she was aware that the orchestra was playing a familiar melody.

"Brett, did you request 'You Light Up My Life'?" she asked.

"No, honest, I didn't. You must have made quite an impression on Mr. Smith the night I asked him to play it for you."

The maestro's touch on the piano keys lent a quality to the song that Joy had never heard before. When he moved his right hand to play the melody on the celeste, the bell-like tones added another dimension that enhanced the impromptu score. From their table Brett and Joy watched the pianist's hands moving gracefully from one instrument to another. Not once did he look at the keyboards, but was constantly scanning the faces of the people in the audience.

When the song had ended, Joy and Brett rose from their table and walked over to thank the pianist.

"Mr. Smith," Joy began, "of all the people who have enjoyed your music, how did you ever remember *us?*"

The orchestra leader's eyes twinkled. "People are my hobby," he said. "I enjoy trying to put faces and tunes together. Bringing pleasure to others is a real source of satisfaction for me. Then, of course," he added, maintaining the melody with one hand while including the band members with a sweep of the other, "I have a great group of musicians who do an outstanding job of improvisation."

"Well, it certainly does a lot for the ego to be remembered. Thanks again for giving us such a beautiful memory." Joy flashed a brilliant smile as Brett bowed, giving a smart salute to the other members of the band.

"It was our pleasure. If you have another song you want to hear, just let me know," Smith said as his hands moved across the keyboard, never missing a beat.

At their table, Joy turned to study the now-familiar face in profile as Brett listened to the music. Questions wandered about, unchecked, in her head. What would it be like to be married to Brett? How would it feel to "belong" to someone? She realized that she was one of the few women her age who had never experienced the ultimate expression of love, and at times she bitterly resented those friends who did not believe her. She had clung tenaciously to that principle of her faith, though, in recent days, the temptation to yield to Brett's ardor had been almost overwhelming.

As she pondered, she knew that she had already made up her mind that she wanted to live with Brett for the rest of her life. She should have told him that she would marry him, but a niggling doubt always managed to creep in just when she was on the brink of decision.

Her thoughts were interrupted when she heard Brett say, "Mmmm, you smell good tonight. Is that a new perfume?"

"I'm glad you noticed," she colored beneath her light tan. "Yes, it is, and I hope it will haunt you like your sandalwood has haunted me."

"I didn't know you liked sandalwood," he said with surprise.

"Only when *you* are wearing it, and only when you are here with me," she stated emphatically.

Brett's arm was now resting on the table. He draped the other casually around the back of his chair as he turned to talk with Joy.

He did not touch her. In fact, his chair was a full two feet away. But as he continued his conversation, she looked into his eyes, the color shifting from bronze to amber and back to rich mahogany. It was as if his eyes were a thing apart, beckoning her, inviting her to lose herself in their warm depths.

As they sparkled and scintillated, they began to move across her face slowly in an almost tangible caress—first to one eye; then, to the other, skimming the tip of her delicate nose, then dropping to linger on the sweet curve of her lips. She could almost feel his lips on hers—warm, firm, desirous. Though she didn't hear a word he was saying, she was held captive by those searching, probing eyes.

They shifted to her jawline, stroking the tender curve of her cheek, moving to touch the hollow at the base of her throat. She felt herself feeling strangely breathless. How incredible. The man had not laid a hand on her, yet she felt the physical warmth of his embrace—and a rising excitement yet to be named. It was an electrifying moment—unlike anything Joy had ever experienced.

When the music ended, breaking the spell, she felt both regret and relief. She excused herself from the table and hurried to the powder room to compose herself. She splashed cold water on her burning face and held her wrists under the faucet, allowing the cooling flow to still her racing pulse. She felt as if she had run a marathon race.

When she returned to the table, Brett rose to seat her, concerned that she might have become ill.

"Did I say anything to cause you to leave so suddenly?" he asked. "I've wracked my brain, but I couldn't imagine how a recital of dull facts about my childhood could have upset you!"

"It really wasn't anything you said, Brett," Joy assured him. "Maybe someday I'll tell you—when I understand it better myself."

CHAPTER 12

THE WORLD HAD NEVER been brighter than it appeared to Joy the following morning when she awakened. Glistening droplets of dew clung to the grass. With the eye of an artist, Joy's mind transformed the scene into a dress of white moiré silk that would shimmer and change as light caught the wavy patterns. Never without a note pad nearby, she recorded her impressions to incorporate later into a dress design.

Suddenly her thoughts returned to her conversation with Ellen about the Debutante Ball. She had not been able to create a design for April Munroe. April would look stunning in a white moiré gown. Aha! she thought. That was the answer to one of the gowns that had been baffling her for so long.

Beauty filled her eyes wherever she looked that morning. The Banyan tree's waxy leaves glimmered in the early morning sunlight. Was this the same view she had seen only yesterday morning? How could one's attitude and state of mind alter so drastically the appearance of things?

Standing before the open window, she breathed in great gulps of air and the fragrances that greeted her were as lovely as the sights. The lingering scent of the night-blooming jasmine near her window was now a romantic and lovely aroma. Only yesterday it had brought tears to her eyes. *What a difference a day makes,* she thought—trite, maybe, but so very true.

Exhilarated, she hurried into the bathroom and stepped into the shower. As the refreshing spray hit her face and then pelted her back, she began to hum. The hum progressed to a "tra la la." Before she knew it she was singing . . . happy songs, love songs, fun songs. Her spirits soared.

With thirty minutes remaining before she was to meet Brett for breakfast, she would still be able to dress leisurely. Reflecting on the events of the evening before, she remembered that Brett had told her he had a business meeting tonight and wouldn't be able to have dinner with her. "If I have to leave day after tomorrow, I want to make the most of every minute we have together," she said aloud. "After breakfast, I'll complete some sketches. This is the first time in months that I've been excited about working."

Deciding that she would go to the beach and sketch after breakfast, she selected a bright watermelon pink swimsuit with grass-green laces that secured the deep plunging front of the suit. She had asked one of the seamstresses to make her a simple boat-necked top and a wrap skirt in grass green, trimmed with the same watermelon shade as the suit. Slices of watermelons were appliqued on both the skirt and the top. It was a nice cover to wear to the dining room, and could be easily removed for swimming and sunbathing.

Joy doubted that wrap skirts would ever drift into complete disfavor with the average homemaker or working woman. They were so comfortable and convenient for quick trips to the supermarket or other errands. She made a mental note to be sure to have plenty of unusual wraps in the boutique for the summer.

She stashed all of her art supplies in a big tote bag, added a towel, and was ready for the day. She had wasted so much time while Brett was away. Today she would make up for all of those unhappy and unproductive days, she promised herself.

Brett was already seated at a table when she entered the dining room. He was intently watching something outside the windows and did not see her until the maitre d' had escorted her to his table.

"What is so interesting out there this morning?" she asked.

"I was just admiring the shuttle yacht, *Mizner's Dream,* in the marina. Why haven't we ridden it to the Beach Club yet?"

"I think it only sails during the daytime. I'm going to the beach after breakfast, so I'll try it out," Joy replied.

"Wish I could go with you and we could just soak up sun all day." He looked wistfully in the direction of the ocean.

"Nope, not today. This morning is going to be all work and little play for me. I intend to accomplish a great deal today. I feel inspired!"

"I'm glad to hear that, and Ellen certainly will be, too, from what you told me about her crisis call. But, besides the dresses for the Debutante Ball, what's the rush?" Brett inquired. "I thought the charity balls were almost a year away."

"I wondered that, too, when Mother would start working on the new gowns almost as soon as the completed ones had been delivered. But since each dress is an original, it takes a lot of time to create just the right design for each client. Then the fabric must be located and purchased.

"Even the trims can be frustrating beyond belief. Several times I have had to change designs completely because none of the suppliers had an item in stock!" Joy tried to explain in layman's terms all of the intricasies of designing, obtaining the materials, and making the patterns to fit the individual. Only then could the dressmakers begin the actual construction and fitting of the garments.

"Good grief! I had no idea dress-designing was so complicated. When you come down to it, it is very much like architecture, isn't it? We design the building, specify all materials to be used, and see that the structure is built properly. Guess we are in the same line of work when you think about it," Brett observed.

"Hey, you know, you're right!" Joy turned to the waiter who was dispensing croissants, muffins, Danish pastries, and other delicacies from a huge metal warmer which hung around his neck. "I think I'll have another of those bran muffins." The waiter lifted out one of the toasty warm muffins with his tongs and placed it on her bread-and-butter plate.

Brett's eyes crinkled with merriment. "Joy, watching you eat is almost as much fun as eating my own meal. I remember when I was a little boy visiting my grandfather, it seemed that everything he ate appeared to taste better than whatever I was eating. He could make a biscuit with butter and syrup look like the treat of a lifetime."

Joy laughed at the thought of Brett as a small boy and finished her bowl of strawberries, selected from a table containing fruits of all descriptions. The waiter brought her broiled fish with grilled tomatoes and potatoes and refilled her coffee cup.

"You can have your fish for breakfast. Just give me good old country ham and eggs. By the way, can you cook?" he asked as an afterthought.

"I'll have you know that I'm a very good cook. Those frozen dinners are a cinch. Just poke them in the oven, set the timer, and voila—instant dinner!" she smiled impishly.

"You have to be kidding! I had enough of those when Mother and Dad would go out to dinner, and leave us kids with the old TV-dinner routine. Seriously, can you cook—I mean good old 'down-home' Southern cooking?" His face had become very solemn as he waited for her reply.

Joy laughed at his anguished expression. "I'm teasing, of course. I enjoy cooking the good old stand-bys like fried chicken, rice and gravy, and grits. Mother taught me when I was just a little girl. She was excellent in the kitchen as well as a talented artist, businesswoman, and an especially good wife and mother. I always hoped I could be like her some-day." Joy's face revealed the pride and love she felt for her mother, as well as a wistful expression of hope for her own future.

"I wanted to be sure that you could cook. If you had to eat in a restaurant all of your life, it would take a millionaire just to pay for your meals!" Brett laughed, knowing that she would be indignant.

"Enough about my appetite! You don't turn down much food yourself, I've noticed," Joy frowned in mock anger.

"Uh, oh! I did say that I wouldn't tease you anymore. By the way, Joy, I'm sorry that I can't have dinner with you tonight. But don't forget to eat," he reminded her. "I don't want you wasting away again."

"Do you really have to go to a business meeting tonight? I have to catch the early flight out day after tomorrow to go back to Atlanta," she asked, secretly hoping that he would cancel his plans.

"I'm afraid so. It's something that can't wait," he stated firmly and her face mirrored her disappointment.

"Well, I'll probably just stop in the Court of Four Lions

and have a bite after I get through with today's sketches. Have a good day . . . I'll miss you." Her voice softened.

"I'll miss you, too, Princess. You take care, hear?" Brett said as he left her to finish her coffee.

When she reached the beach, Joy removed her skirt and top and walked into the surf to test the temperature of the water. Finding it a little too cool for an early morning swim, she returned to the lounge chair with its canvas awning which she could use later to block the sun. She stretched out on the lounge and stared at the ocean. Her creative mind went to work at once, conjuring the vision of a dress that would capture some of the beauty of the Atlantic.

Quickly she unpacked her materials and sketched a long dress of ombre chiffon in shades of greens and blues. Diagonal rows of ruffles extended from one shoulder downward to the floor-length hemline, giving the appearance of waves rolling toward the beach. She added a long, sheer shawl of the same fabric. It added an ethereal quality to the dress when draped around the throat in front, and when the wearer walked, the fabric would float softly in her wake.

And I know just the woman to wear it, she thought. No one would look better in it than Doris Key. Her naturally blonde hair would shine like the sun coming up over the ocean. That was it! Doris would look like Botticelli's Venus. Unlike Venus, however, she would be clothed in a gown the color of the sea. Excitement mounted as she gazed around the shoreline for other inspirations.

She walked down the beach and found a long, white feather, probably from one of the seagulls that followed the boats which plied the inlet, she thought. Looking at the feather, she sketched a mental picture of a long, black

135

strapless taffeta dress with no ornamentation except for one extraordinary white feather which would be fashioned from organza. It would be tacked across the bodice diagonally with only the tip of the feather extending above the bodice. Ah, perfect! Simple, but elegant.

Hurrying back to her lounge chair, she captured the image on paper, along with a long flowing gown of creamy, sand-colored georgette, sprinkled with beads the colors of the small shells that lay strewn over the beach.

Her hands moved rapidly now as she concocted a pale gold dress with a handkerchief skirt that emulated the now-endangered sea oats which waved so gracefully in the ocean breeze. Those little points of the skirt, if made of soft chiffon, would ripple with movement—giving the appearance of sea oats swaying gently. As she put the final touches to the dress, she smiled broadly.

To clear her head, Joy raced into the ocean and dived into a wave. She rose exuberantly to catch another huge wave, riding it almost to the beach. Childlike, she rushed back and forth as if she might miss one moment of the wondrous experience.

Finally, exhausted from her exertion, she struggled out of the water and shook her golden head. Vibrant energy replaced the depression that had drained her and left her listless.

Joy strolled along the beach, letting her body dry in the warm breeze. She stooped to pick up a shell and stared at it thoughtfully, turning it around and around in her hand. *How very beautiful,* she thought. *I wonder where this shell began its long journey?*

The beauty of the shell inspired yet another idea for a dress. It must be a strapless dress, she decided, and the fabric would stand away slightly from the body at the top. Satin—that would be the only fabric to duplicate the sheen of the shell. But it had to be lined with satin as well. Yes, the dress would be shell pink, and the lining which would peek above the top of the bodice would be a deeper shade of pink, just like the inside of the shell she was holding. A vision of the skirt took shape in her imagination. It would be long in the back and curve gradually upward to knee-length in the front so that the deep pink lining could be seen. Delighted with her final idea, Joy ran back to sketch the dress. Afterward she relaxed contentedly in the sun.

When her hearty appetite surfaced once more, she walked to the Cabana Terrace for a quick bite of lunch—her reward for a successful morning's work. Long ago Joy had decided that, even if she were dieting, she would never skip breakfast. Her body craved some nourishment when she awakened so that she could have enough energy for the day. If she missed any meal, it would have to be lunch. Then she tried to have dinner early enough so that she would have time to work off some of the calories before going to bed. She was able to keep her weight under control with this routine, or by cutting down the size of the portions.

Leisurely she enjoyed the fresh seafood salad and entertained herself with her favorite pastime—people-watching. A little boy about four years old walked toward the nearby pool. She couldn't help but notice his dark brown eyes and his sturdy, little legs. He could have been a miniature of Brett, she decided. Should she and Brett marry and have children, their little boys would all have legs like that—and large, chocolate-brown eyes!

Did she know Brett well enough to marry him? What would she say if he asked her again? Her outburst the night that he had proposed had certainly been enough to discourage any man, especially after the way she had responded to his kisses on the beach. Yes, he had every right to have been angry and confused. And why had she not told him that she would marry him when he returned from Atlanta?

She wanted Brett. She needed him. He had become a part of her life, and the thought of losing him was unbearable. Just how long would he wait for her to make up her mind? Surely even his patience had a limit. Perhaps she should just tell him that she wanted to be his wife.

That wouldn't really be proposing to him, since he had already asked her to marry him. Things were completely different now. Yet she hesitated. Perhaps she was still playing the role of a Southern lady of an earlier era.

She certainly didn't agree with many of the ideas her friends held. Quite a few of them considered her peculiar because she already felt equal to men and saw no need for legislation to guarantee that equality. In some ways she felt that the scale tipped in the direction of women, giving them a favored position. She liked the idea of men opening doors for her, helping her with her coat, pulling out her chair, and paying for dinner or the theatre. No, she didn't want to be subservient, but she did like the respect and protection of men. Brett gave her the impression of cherishing her without dominating her. Was there another man like him in the whole world?

He had made it perfectly clear that he wanted to know when Joy was ready to marry him. *I'll just have to call him tonight when he gets back from his meeting and say, "I'm ready for you to ask me,"* she thought. *No, that doesn't sound right. Oh well! By tonight, I'll think of something.*

CHAPTER 13

THERE SEEMED LITTLE NEED to dress for dinner, but Joy had promised Brett. At the last minute she decided to dine in the Patio Royale, where she could enjoy the music of the orchestra rather than in the Court of Four Lions, where she would have only her own thoughts to keep her company.

Since she would not be seeing Brett that evening, Joy took no particular pains with her dress. She grabbed a simple long-sleeved shirtwaist, applied transparent powder to tone down her sunburned face, some mascara, and a touch of lipstick. Running a brush through her hair, she noticed that it was at least two shades lighter. She would have to be more careful in the sun tomorrow.

As she walked through the lobby, she spoke to Domenick who was openly appreciative of the lovely girl in the sapphire blue dress. The color made her eyes sparkle like pale blue crystals, and her face glowed with pleasure when she saw her old friend.

Once again she was grateful that the hotel had not abandoned some of the timeless traditions of service. There was something so coldly impersonal about self-service which had replaced such personnel as the bell captain and bellmen in many of the large hotel chains. It was unthinkable, in her mind, that there should not be a Domenick who remembered the names of guests from former days and was now welcoming their children. Joy decided that there was something inherent in her being that resisted such progress as the building of condos and the self-operated elevators. She wondered if she would be considered a "maverick" had she lived out West rather than in the South. And why should she change for the sake of change, even if hers was not a popular stand—or even if it was in opposition to Brett's?

She studied the menu. Brett would have loved hearing her order, she thought. Ah, but she could almost taste the marinated zucchini sticks with Genoa salami and the chilled melon and fruit soup. Her mouth watered in anticipation. She smiled to herself. *Joy, you are becoming an impossible 'foodaholic.'*

The music, as on previous evenings, was varied enough to please all of the diners, and its quality was unmatched. Joy had grown to love dining while listening to live music. Like Mr. Smith, each of the musicians seemed to enjoy bringing pleasure to the guests.

When the entreé was served, Joy had tasted only a few bites when she glanced toward the orchestra once more. As her eyes shifted, she caught sight of a familiar figure being seated at a table just in front of the orchestra. Startled, she jerked her head back in that direction. It was Brett! And he was not alone. Seated with him was a gorgeous strawberry blonde. So this was the business that "couldn't wait."

I've seen that girl somewhere before . . . Joy struggled to remember. *But where? I know—it was the day I had lunch with Marianna!*

Heartsick, Joy slumped in her chair, fearful that Brett would spot her. She had believed every word he had told her. Yet here he was with another woman only hours after his passionate declaration of love! What's more—he had probably been seeing her all along. Anger and indignation seethed within.

Though her first inclination had been to bolt and run, her instinctive curiosity outweighed the decision. She shifted a little lower into her chair so that she could study the couple. There was little chance that Brett would see her, however, because his eyes were riveted on the woman's face. And he was not by himself.

All of the men at surrounding tables were casting appreciative glances at her. Men who were not with female companions stared unashamedly at the gorgeous creature. *Men!* Joy thought. *They're all alike!*

The woman with Brett could have been a high-fashion model if judged by her face alone. Her figure was equally devastating. Reddish-blonde hair fell in shining waves around her shoulders. And the shoulders that it brushed were bare. *Too bare,* Joy thought. Her dress was a simple, black affair with tiny spaghetti straps. Joy gritted her teeth as she watched the woman who was now laughing at something that Brett had said.

He was undeniably charming. *Keep 'em laughing, Brett. That's your motto, isn't it? But you made your big mistake tonight,* Joy thought bitterly. *You thought that I would be having dinner in the Court of Four Lions, so I would never find out about your little tête-á-tête, didn't you? Well, tonight your plan backfired!*

Then the anger that had erupted began to turn to self-pity. Tears welled in Joy's eyes. *Brett just used me and then tossed me aside when he saw something more interesting,* she grieved. Tears coursed down her face, and she grabbed the coral linen napkin and tried to staunch the flow.

With a terrible sense of timing, the waiter appeared to ask Joy if she were not feeling well or if her scallopini were not to her liking. Through her sobs Joy managed to convey that the food was just fine, but that she felt a little ill. It was true. She was sick with humiliation!

She asked the waiter for the check, suddenly eager to escape the sight of Brett and his lovely dinner companion. He reached into the breast pocket of his jacket and produced the bill. As he did so, he asked solicitously if there were anything that he could do to help. Joy bit her tongue. It was a temptation to tell him what he could do to the couple who were now dancing to the music that she had been enjoying only moments before. She would like to see the entire plate of scallopini dumped over Brett's head! Instead, she nodded negatively and signed the check.

Knowing that she would have to traverse the entire length of the dining room to get to the nearest exit, she looked for the darkest and quickest route. The last thing she wanted was for Brett to see her. She would never give him the satisfaction of knowing how he had upset her. He and the woman were seated at their table again, and the route she had chosen would take her directly into his line of vision. Well, she would just have to leave as inconspicuously as possible.

Mustering all of her courage, she rose and turned her head toward the wall. Maybe Brett wouldn't recognize her from the back. The distance seemed interminable—like miles before she reached the door. Outside, she hurried down the brightly carpeted steps that led into the lobby. *I made it!* she thought with relief.

Unexpectedly a hand touched her shoulder. She jumped. Then Brett had his arms around her. He really had nerve to follow her as if nothing had happened! Joy seethed with anger. She tried to push his arms away, but she could not speak. Struggling to break his hold on her, she glanced at his eyes and wondered why she could have been struck both deaf and dumb when she looked into them.

"Joy, honey, what's wrong?" Brett asked. "Where have you been? I've tried to reach you all day. I even tried your room just before coming here. Have you eaten? Come on back and sit with me while I finish my meal, will you?"

She stared at him in disbelief. Did he suppose that she hadn't seen him and *that woman?* Did he really expect her to follow him meekly and be a fifth wheel to their cozy little twosome? Words continued to fail her.

"Joy, what in the world is wrong with you? Are you sick or something? I just wanted you to come in and sit with Sam and me while we have dinner." His face showed no evidence of repentance.

Then all of the words that had remained trapped spewed forth with unexpected venom. "You expect me to go and sit with you and your date while the two of you have dinner! You were the one who had such an important *business meeting* tonight! Business, hah! And I believed you when you told me that you loved me and wanted to marry me. Then the minute my back is turned, you are dancing with a strawberry-blonde bombshell! Well, Brett, you have done one good thing for me—no, two. First, I have finally gotten my spunk back after a very long time. And, second, I won't ever trust another man as long as I live!"

"Hold it! Hold it!" Brett interrupted her tirade. "I said that I wanted you to meet *Sam*. That 'strawberry-blonde bombshell,' as you call her, is *Samantha*—'Sam' for short. She's one of the engineers on the condo job. When I told her that I hated not being with you tonight, she insisted that the three of us have dinner together. We could talk business, and I could still be with you. Now, does that smooth your

143

ruffled feathers a little? Sam really is a very nice lady. And by the way, she is very much married.''

His long dissertation had given Joy time to weigh the situation. His explanation sounded plausible. Then she asked weakly, ''But why didn't you ever tell me that Sam was a *woman?*''

''Honestly, honey, the thought never occurred to me. She is just an engineer as far as I'm concerned. After I met you, do you think I could be interested in another woman, even if she *were* available?'' He smiled down at her and kissed the tip of her sunburned nose. Joy's anger melted, to be replaced with utter contrition.

''You are really rotten to the core!'' she stormed at him in mock indignation. ''Do you realize that I wasn't able to eat my veal scallopini after I saw you with her? I wasted all of that good food, plus my baked eggplant!''

Brett threw back his head and laughed heartily. Then he countered, ''Now I know the way to your heart. Come on back with me. Never let it be said that you left the table without finishing a meal on my account.''

He put his arm around her waist possessively and guided her back to the table where Sam sat alone. When she saw them, Sam's face lighted with pleasure.

''At last I get to meet the 'Joy' of Brett's life,'' she said with sincerity. ''He has talked about you so much that it would have been a shame not to have met you.''

Joy could not help but warm to the woman's friendly smile and pleasant personality. Brett proceeded to tell Sam about Joy's misconceptions about her and soon they were all laughing.

''This certainly isn't the first time that my name has gotten me in trouble,'' Sam commented. ''Many a wife has stared holes through me before they realize that I am strictly an engineer when I'm at work. Breaking up other relationships just isn't my style. My mother and father were divorced because of 'the other woman' and I go out of my way to keep associations with other men on a professional level. It is hard enough, at times, to be a woman engineer without having my name cause problems, too.''

Joy smiled at her and said, ''Well, I'm certainly glad that you're happily married. I'd hate to have you as my competition. You outshine everyone around.''

''Not in Brett's eyes. I don't think he even realized that I was a woman until Frank broke the news that I would be taking a leave of absence soon to have a baby.'' Sam's reassuring smile calmed any lingering fears.

The conversation was mostly happy talk regarding the arrival of the new baby and Joy's work. Then the two women teased Brett unmercifully about his near-fatal error in neglecting to tell Joy that Sam was a woman. Being outnumbered, he changed the subject to the construction of the condo.

While Brett and Sam discussed business, Joy reflected on what Sam had said. So Brett had meant it when he told Joy that she was the only woman in the world for him. Well, after tonight, she would have to make sure that he asked her again to marry him. There was no longer any question what her answer would be.

CHAPTER 14

AFTER THEY HAD DRIVEN Sam home and Joy had promised to keep in touch, Brett swung the car around and headed up A1A. Joy struggled not to comment as they passed the high-rise buildings that hugged the shoreline. She wanted to avoid another controversy about the buildings. Instead, she asked Brett what made him decide to study architecture and why he had chosen Auburn instead of Georgia Tech, which was so close to home.

"Well, to tell the truth, I needed to get away from home. Cut the apron strings, you know. Auburn has a good school of architecture. Several of my friends were there, and, besides, I really did want the chance to play football with "Shug" Jordan as my coach. As it turned out, I didn't get to play too much because I happened to be on campus when Pat Sullivan and Terry Beasley had their 'dynamic duo' going. Since I played the same position that Terry played, I sat on the bench most of the season. But I'm not complaining. They worked well together."

"They were something else, weren't they?" Joy interjected. "I was so happy when Pat got the Heisman Trophy. But when Auburn beat Alabama by a score of 17-16 with two blocked punts, you must have been going crazy down there!"

"Hey, Love, you've been holding out on me. How does such a feminine little thing know so much about football?" Brett asked in disbelief.

"I've loved football since I was a little girl," she explained. "My father took me to my brother's Little League football practices every afternoon. Even in high school I was an oddity because I really enjoyed the games. My girl friends were never able to understand it. But tell me more! What was it like when Auburn beat Alabama?" Joy's interested questioning was all Brett needed.

"Pandemonium broke out all over the state. Records of the last few minutes of the ballgame were broadcast from a loudspeaker at the front of the bookstore. Toomers' Corner, the main intersection in front of the campus, was a madhouse. It was Mardi Gras, the Fourth of July, and New Year's Eve, all rolled up into one! When we got back to the campus, the party was still going strong. For days, as I worked in the architecture building, I could look out and see streamers hanging from all of the old oaks, magnolias, and telephone lines. Samford Hall, the main building, looked like a Christmas tree covered with tinsel.

"The guys who lived in Alabama were more excited than anyone else because of the big cross-state rivalry. But every year I just hope that Auburn beats Tech and those Georgia Bulldogs. Then I don't have to take the teasing from all of the folks in Atlanta. . . . Hey!" he exclaimed, looking over at her. "I order two season tickets every year for the games at Auburn. Would you like to go this fall? It would be fun showing you the campus and being able to talk football with my date rather than having to explain everything that is happening on the field.'' Brett was intrigued with Joy's interest in the game he loved—and delighted to discover that they had something else in common.

"I'd love to! I haven't seen too many games since Bill was killed. Now that my father is gone, I usually watch the games on TV or go by myself. I haven't found a woman who shares my love for football and, unfortunately, the man I was engaged to went to the games only if he were trying to impress someone.'' She thought about John and realized that there was no trace of bitterness. Changing the subject, she said, "Why don't you try your hand at coaching Little League football? You would be great with kids, I bet.''

"I've thought about it, but my schedule is so crazy that I can't be there early enough for practice. And when I have to go out of town, I would have to miss practice completely. It really wouldn't be fair to the kids. But I owe a lot to my Little League coach.'' Brett stopped and turned to Joy, a look of incredulity on his face as realization dawned.

"Bill Lawrence must have been your brother! Joy, I had not made the connection until just now! I played football with him in Little League and, later, in high school. And you were the kid sister who always came to watch him practice. Now I remember you! You had chubby, little legs and big, blue eyes, and the same happy smile you have now. Everyone called you 'Kitten,' probably because you were so cute and cuddly. How could I have forgotten?''

Joy's face was illumined with instant recognition. "Then that's why *your* name was so familiar to me! I kept wondering why the name 'McCort' kept coming back to me. But you weren't called 'Brett' then. Didn't they call you 'Buddy'?''

Brett threw back his head and laughed. "You're right! And if I hadn't put my foot down and demanded that the family start calling me 'Brett,' I would have one day been

148

known as 'Grandpa Buddy.' Can you picture that?''

Joy felt a slight blush burn her face as she said, ''But you still don't know the whole story. I had the worst crush on you then, and you didn't even know that I was alive. I pestered Bill constantly to invite you over to the house. But when you came, you ignored me like the plague.''

''Well, Honey, I must have been blind. Of course, the age difference did mean a lot back when I was all of fourteen or fifteen and you must have been only eight or nine. Now, I know why I waited all these years to find the right girl. I had been waiting for that little 'Kitten' to grow up.'' Brett smiled at her, and she felt a warm, pleasurable sensation sweep through her body.

She had found a link with the past that had been stored in her attic of memories for so many years. He and Bill had been good friends, and their families had enjoyed sharing their sons' athletic accomplishments. It was natural that, with the passing of years, they had grown apart until they had lost all track of each other. How incredible that she had known Brett all these years, only to find her 'first love' again in Boca.

The rest of the drive was spent in comfortable silence as they reviewed the past. Soon Brett was turning into El Camino Real and they were back at the Cloister. After he had left the car with the parking attendant, he took Joy's arm and steered her toward the fountain.

''Now, we are going to sit and enjoy the fountain tonight and forget that other unhappy scene,'' he said firmly.

This is the time, Joy thought happily. Surely he would ask her now. They sat on the same bench where Joy had shed so many tears on that other dreadful night. But this was a new and beautiful beginning. She would not spoil it.

Brett put his arms around her and kissed her tenderly.

Then she heard her own voice murmuring, ''Brett, I love

you so much.'' Had she really said the words? Had he heard her? The answer to her questions was instantaneous.

Brett grasped her shoulders and looked into her eyes. ''Do you really mean that, Joy? Look at me and tell me again.''

When she stared into his dark brown hypnotic eyes, her heart began its accelerated thumping. The pounding moved upward into her throat. She knew she was on the verge of making what might be a binding commitment, and fear swept her once again. But this time she squelched the apprehension.

''I do love you, Brett,'' she said firmly as his stunned expression changed to one of overwhelming relief and love.

Without a word he grasped her to him as if he would never let her go. She could feel his heart bearing like a tom-tom, matching the wild rhythm of her own. The strong arms that enveloped her were like balm to her aching heart. His strength flowed into her own veins. He was the shelter she had found in the 'winter of her life,' like the promise of the cherry blossom. He was her Banyan tree, her friend, her link to the past and to the future. He was her first love—and her last—the one God had chosen for her.

Having breakfast with Brett the following morning, Joy feasted on his eyes, his face, his smile. Her appetite had not lessened. Instead, the beautiful new feeling that existed between them enhanced the flavor of her food and renewed her zest for living.

Happily she told him her plans for her last day in Boca. As she enumerated the things that she hoped to accomplish, his eyebrows rose in astonishment.

''Whoa! How in the world are you going to do all of that in only one day? Are you sure that you can't stay a little longer?'' he pleaded.

"Brett, there is nothing I would like more than to stay here at the Cloister with you. But Ellen needs me, and I can't let her down. Will you be coming to Atlanta soon?"

"I certainly hope so. Pete Jennings seems to be feeling better. When his leg heals, he can take over the project here. By the way, will you have dinner with me tonight? It may be our last for quite a while," he said with a touch of unhappiness.

"What a perfect ending to my visit. I'll be ready whenever you say," Joy replied.

It was she who left the dining room first that morning. So many things remained to be done that she knew she must not waste a minute. Now that Brett was back, she felt a strong resurgence of life and creative energy. Her step was buoyant and her heart light as she walked away.

Joy hurried into the Mizner Garden with its two huge fountains embellished with the colorfully decorated tiles. Each in its own way was a work of art, but her favorite would always be the Lady of Boca's fountain, she decided.

The flowers that surrounded her gave her the same inspiration for dress designs as had the ocean and the beach. Quickly she sketched a dress that gave the impression of a poinsettia. Ruffles made from a series of triangles formed layers of pointed petals which stood away from the floor-length straight scarlet skirt.

The Jacaranda tree with its lavender blossoms called to mind a pale orchid taffeta with a bell-shaped skirt and a whisper of a pale green sash just as soft as the fern-like leaves of the tree.

The yellow hibiscus with its rich green foliage inspired a green chiffon formal with a high neck in front and low in the back, with soft folds of fabric falling from the shoulders to the waist where a large, silk yellow hibiscus flower would be attached.

But then she looked at the bougainvillea and her imagination drew from the blooming vine the most elegant dress of all. With this dress she would capture the charm of the Old World as Addison Mizner had when he built the Cloister. The gown would be a traditional Spanish dress as worn by the original flamenco dancers, the Andelusian gypsies, hugging the body to the knees. There, a bouffant ruffle would fall to the floor giving room for the dancer to move her feet freely. The fabric would be fuschia taffeta overlaid with sheer white lace, revealing the bright color beneath. To complete the look, she would use a tall Spanish comb for the hair. From this comb would fall a mantilla of white lace which would be attached by tiny, fuschia silk blossoms that would emulate the bougainvillea blooms. *Maybe this will be my very own dress,* she thought, *to remind me of the beginning of a new life.*

She put her sketch pad away and rushed back into the lobby, remembering the skirt she had seen in DeLoy's. Perhaps it was still there. Though it was a rare occurrence when she bought clothes from other shops, she wanted the lovely creation to wear to dinner with Brett.

She rushed into the boutique and tried on the skirt. It was a perfect fit! But she needed a blouse to complete the ensemble. Instantly her eye was drawn to a pale turquoise design, with a single soft layer of ruffles at the neck and down the front of the blouse.

Brett would love it! But would he sweep her into his arms and ask her to marry him tonight? Suddenly she was impatient to see him. She had never been more sure of any decision in her life.

Her shopping adventure could not have been more successful. When Brett saw her in the rainbow skirt and turquoise blouse, he let out a long, low whistle of approval. He put his arm around her waist, holding her close to him, as they followed the maitre d' to their table that evening.

For the first time since she had known Brett, she ordered her meal without thought for the tempting selections on the menu. Butterflies fluttered in her stomach in anticipation of the question which would decide her future.

To her dismay, as the meal progressed, Brett chatted about mundane things—his work, the boutique, the weather. Nothing at all was said about their relationship. In fact she might have been having a conversation with a perfect stranger. With each course, her brilliant smile faded until, by the time the entrée was served, her spirits had drooped.

The Smith orchestra was playing in the dining room that evening. Again, the strains of the lovely melody that had come to have such a special meaning for them rippled through the room. Brett moved toward her and kissed her lightly on the cheek. Joy held her breath. If he were going to ask her, now was the opportune time. But once more she was disappointed. They listened in silence.

When the band completed the medley they were playing, the audience applauded appreciatively. Joy tried to keep her smile firmly in place, but the effort was becoming almost too much. The waiter asked if he could remove her plate which still contained half of her main course. She nodded miserably.

When he picked up the plate, she saw it! Tucked under one corner of the plate lay a pale blue velvet box! She looked at Brett questioningly. A faint smile played on his lips. But he said nothing.

She picked up the box and opened it. There, nestled in a bed of white satin, was the most beautiful pear-shaped diamond ring she had ever seen. She gasped.

"Honey," Brett said, "I was afraid to ask you to marry me again, so I decided to let the ring do it for me. Before you run away or tell me to wait, I'm going to try once more. Joy, will you marry me as soon as I can get back to Atlanta? I love you and need you with me for the rest of my life."

"Oh, Brett, I was so afraid you wouldn't ask me again! Yes, yes, yes! I'll marry you! Whenever you say!" The sparkling tears in Joy's eyes rivaled the brilliance of the diamond that Brett had slipped on her finger.

Joy's voice quivered with emotion as she looked at her hand which was now adorned with the beautiful ring. "Brett, there is a quotation that keeps running through my mind when I'm with you. I hope I can remember it because it must have been intended for just this moment. 'I love you, not only for what you are, but for what I am when I am with you.'"

Brett held her hands in his as he responded, "And I love you for lighting my life and giving it new meaning . . . Now, there are two things you need to do when you get home. Reserve the church, and call the seamstress and tell her you have a rush job. Your very first design *has* to be your wedding dress. We will do this up in fine style because it is going to be the *only wedding* either of us will ever have. Understood?"

"Understood!" she replied.

The following morning Joy said her goodbyes to some of the hotel employees who had been especially kind to her. When she spoke to Domenick, she promised him that she wouldn't stay away so long. Perhaps, Joy mused, Brett would even surprise her with a honeymoon trip to Boca— where they could begin their own family tradition.

She stood for a moment, savoring again the elegant surroundings, grateful that the beauty of the grand old hotel was not merely a facade, but a spirit, offering refuge and loving concern to the weary travelers who entered its doors. Some of them were looking for physical rest and a change of pace. Others, like herself, were looking for something far more significant. She had been so right to come here to recover the love and security of her childhood. In doing so she had found once more the security of God's perfect love. It was as though He were saying, *My child, now you know the meaning of real joy—and Brett is only one sign of my love for you. I will be with you always . . .*

Brett stood patiently waiting for her to board the airport limousine. His reluctance to let her go showed clearly in his countenance. When he kissed her, she clung to him, fearful that leaving him would break the spell. But as he released her, his warm smile and the love in his eyes told her eloquently that their reunion would be forever.

"Don't forget! You'd look beautiful in a burlap bag, but your wedding dress is a priority." he reminded, as he closed the door of the car.

Looking back through a veil of happy tears at this man who would belong to her until death parted them, Joy spotted the fountain beyond. "The Lady," clothed in sunlight, seemed to glow with an ethereal splendor. The source of her smile would forever remain a mystery, but Joy suspected that she was pleased with the events that had transpired under her watchful eye.

As the sun grew visibly brighter, it touched the cascade of sparkling water flowing from the fountain. Instantly it was transformed in Joy's mind into a shimmering bridal veil, sprinkled with pearls and opalescent crystal beads. The Lady smiled on . . .

MEET THE AUTHORS

VELMA SEAWELL DANIELS has always been passionately in love with books. She is a native of Florida, where she has earned the title of "The Book Lady." She is an NBC television hostess, librarian, book reviewer, newspaper and magazine columnist, and popular seminar and conference speaker. Velma is married to her "first-grade" sweetheart, Dexter, a championship golfer and business executive. Velma writes for *Guideposts* and is the author of three inspirational best-sellers—*Patches of Joy, Kat* (the true story of her calico cat), and *Celebrate Joy*.

PEGGY ESKEW KING grew up in Anderson, South Carolina, where she studied art and fashion design at Winthrop College. She delights in creating and sewing original designs for her personal wardrobe as well as for family and friends. Peggy has won numerous awards, including the title of Mrs. Columbus and runner-up to Mrs. Georgia. She travels extensively and is a voracious reader —logging as many as 400 books per year. Peggy now resides in Winter Haven, Florida, where she welcomes her minister sons and their families for frequent visits.

Serenade Books are inspirational romances in contemporary settings, designed to bring you a joyful, heart-lifting reading experience.

Other Serenade books available in your local bookstore:

#1 ON WINGS OF LOVE, Elaine L. Schulte
#2 LOVE'S SWEET PROMISE, Susan C. Feldhake
#3 FOR LOVE ALONE, Susan C. Feldhake
#4 LOVE'S LATE SPRING, Lydia Heermann
#5 IN COMES LOVE, Mab Graff Hoover
#6 FOUNTAIN OF LOVE, Velma S. Daniels and Peggy E. King.

Watch for the Serenade/Saga Series, historical inspirational romances, to be released in January, 1984.